Into The Purple Duchy

Other books by the Author

Death Train

Golden Giant: Hemlo and the Rush for Canada's Gold

A Viewer's Guide to Halley's Comet

The Male of The Species

Into
The Purple
Duchy

Matthew Hart

KEY PORTER BOOKS

Canadian Cataloguing in Publication Data
Hart, Matthew

Into the purple duchy

ISBN 1-55013-726-3

1. Bismarck (Battleship) — Fiction.   2. Hood (Battle cruiser) — Fiction.   I. Title.

PS8565.A77I5   1995   C813'.54   C95-931627-2
PR9199.3.H37I5   1995

The publisher gratefully acknowledges the assistance of the Canada Council, the Ontario Arts Council and the Ontario Publishing Centre.

The author is grateful for the generous support of the Ontario Arts Council and the Woodcock Fund of The Writers' Development Trust.

Key Porter Books Limited
70 The Esplanade
Toronto, Ontario
Canada M5E 1R2

Printed and bound in Canada

95 96 97 98 99 6 5 4 3 2 1

At 6:01 a.m., 24 May, 1941, the British battle cruiser *Hood*, old and badly armored, blew up and sank off Iceland under fire from the German battleship *Bismarck*. Three days later the Royal Navy caught *Bismarck*, crippled her steering, and sank her with a terrible bombardment.

Once upon a time there was a time that some people say is still going on.

— Cees Nooteboom, *In the Dutch Mountains*

i

BEFORE THE WARSHIPS appeared there was that hard winter. In Canada people wept from the cold. Tears welded their eyelids shut. Cars lay felled along the streets, their tires shattered into bits like shells. Slowly the cities tightened to a standstill. In the countryside whole forests exploded in the frost. In Ontario an archbishop went out on snowshoes, earmuffs clamped to his head beneath his mitre. Acolytes and priests attended him with candles and thuribles, and the tallest, straightest boy preceded him with an eight-foot pole surmounted by a silver cross. "*Ecce Sacerdos magnus,*" chanted the miserable priests: "Behold, the great high priest." When his feet turned numb from cold, the archbishop halted the procession. He raised his crozier in a mittened fist and sketched a cross into blue air. A grove of maples burst into shards before him. He hid his despair behind a level gaze, and asked God how he had sinned. His face was smeared with ice where he tried to wipe his eyes. He returned to his cathedral in defeat.

That winter ended suddenly, bursting in a moment into an exuberant spring. Ruby dawns and sunsets rushed across the sky. Volcanoes in the Philippines were cited for this splendid violence. Each day a cavalry of pigments rode into the sky and shook its warclubs at the clouds. This was how spring arrived, as if to drums, and from this vernal battlefield emerged the ships.

The Americans glimpsed them from a satellite – a pair of dinosaurs afoot in the broad ocean, alive! News of that old war electrified the world. The tidings rippled like banners, people snatched at bulletins. News of the chase gave embassies a chance to send out messages in bursts of code recording the latest rumors, how the ships had appeared off Punta del Este, how the sounds of a duel had floated over Iceland on a westerly, as if the ships were fighting in the Denmark Strait. Cars with pennants raced down streets in Rome and Washington, Paris, London and Berlin. Everyone drank too much. Men put on dinner jackets and arrived at parties late, with worried looks, then hurried off to waiting cars, the pennants, drinks. A perfect time for sex, what with so much heated prose and the posturing of states. People crept about on tiptoe, cranked by excitement, and a glance between a man and woman would explode into a tangle of drenched sheets. This stage passed. It would have to. Damn it, a pair of warships at each other's throats for fifty years!? Come *on*.

ii

DOÑA TERESA STAGGERED as the ship fell sideways in a trough. Still, she did not fall, or even put out her arm. She'd lived aboard for decades, always wore a freshly ironed blouse, a silver locket on a chain, and the kind of expression proper to a condor. Her hair was arranged in tight grey curls around a bony face. What makeup she wore went on in seconds. A lady like this does not much tumble to the deck.

Bismarck bowled along in a quartering sea. It was her worst point of sailing, she slewed across the ocean in an evil corkscrew. Also she was down by the bows, had been for years. Her forward compartments had been holed by gunfire and were not likely now to be pumped out, although the pumps went day and night. It vexed Doña Teresa, but what did not? Take this business with infuriating Wickel.

Oberartilleriemechaniker Wickel held himself stiffly as Doña Teresa came into the galley and aimed her beak at him. Wickel was always stiff: short, red, stiff, and permanently furious. Now he stood by that ridiculous omelette, like a bulldog determined to defend a piece of yellow cardboard. The cook was useless, huddled in a corner with his mates, terrified of Wickel. At Wickel's side stood a man much younger than the rest of them. He wore the uniform of a Kapitänleutnant of the German wartime navy, and looked entirely helpless. Doña Teresa addressed him.

"You must be firm with this person," she indicated Wickel. "He has no rights here. His writ runs elsewhere. Have we no cooks? Has it come to this, that even the cooks give way before him?"

Of course it had come to that. It had come to that for fifty years, as she well knew. Hans-Adam sighed. "It's his latest omelette," he gestured helplessly. "He insists."

Hans-Adam's helplessness arose from the fact that he was thirty-six, and the youngest of the rest of them was twice as old. Doña Teresa knew this, and so what? Wasn't he an officer? It made her mad, plain mad. Hans-Adam would eat anything of Wickel's: omelettes, tortes, those disgusting cookies. And now there was another irritant, a sprout of hair gathered into an elastic band at the back of Hans-Adam's head. This was what came of watching American TV. In spite of Doña Teresa's campaign of blistering sarcasm, Hans-Adam ate what he pleased and would not cut his hair. Bloody TV. Bloody hair. Bloody Wickel.

"I know all *about* his omelettes," Doña Teresa sneered, "and so do the men. They will not have it. They refuse to eat another meal in the form of eggs," she tossed a hand at Wickel. For answer, Wickel seized two eggs, cracked them and sent them into a skillet. He worked amazingly adroitly when you consider that his complement of digits, including thumbs, was five. Defiantly he flipped a toggle switch. A flame snapped to attention beneath the skillet. A handful of spices followed the eggs. A new and alien smell erupted into the galley. Wickel seized a spatula and stirred. The eggs bubbled and turned brown. Two minutes later Wickel folded the mess, once. *Bismarck* shuddered into a mountainous sea. They all hopped about the galley, first on one foot, then the other, hands firmly behind their backs or shoved in pockets, each determined not to be the first to reach for a support. The ship slumped back to an even keel. Wickel stepped to the range and retrieved his trophy. He beamed at it savagely. Hans-Adam stared at it. Doña Teresa kept her eyes averted.

"Smells all right, doesn't it?" Hans-Adam sniffed. "Healthy, too." Doña Teresa met this with a ferrous silence. "I mean," Hans-Adam floundered, "well, eggs."

"Prince," said Doña Teresa, directing a heavy glance at his spurt of hair, "you disappoint me." She transferred her gaze to his eyes and allowed it to remain there, a black stare in which he might read the depths of her chagrin. Only when a blush appeared on his cheek did she consider her visit ended, and with that she spread her wings and coasted off, borne on the rising column of her censure, abandoning Hans-Adam before he could raise that annoying defense of his, the tapping of his fingernail against his teeth or the raising of an eyebrow, or both together. To hell with his bloody arrogance. To hell with omelettes. Doña Teresa had never eaten Wickel's food and never would. She had an appetite for tinned peaches, and happily, a large supply.

iii

IN EARLY APRIL the battleship *Bismarck* came out of the steep Atlantic and ascended the St. Lawrence River. Red with rust and pouring smoke she plodded into the current. A calico of flowers clung to her, thousands of blooms, tens of thousands, purple and pink and mauve and white. They drooped from her superstructure, crawled about the decks. Marvelously hardy — twenty kinds of clematis, or thirty. In some places it clung to a lattice made of pipes that shunted heat in detours from the stack, supplying a warm place for the plants to thrive. Otherwise they'd evolved unaided, as life will, seizing whatever genes get flung its way. The *Clematis montana* was not as pink as landsmen would expect, but rustier. *C. texensis* (Duchess of Albany) had learned to thrive on rotting steel: its blooms looked less like purple throats than warnings printed in vines. You would say the same of yellow Miss Bateman or the shoals of mid-blue General Sikorski — that they were clematis, yes, but something else as well.

At *Bismarck*'s water-line she wore a skirt of living weeds that fanned out from her hull. A head like a seal's (it was a seal) poked out of this lavish habitat and surveyed the shore of Anticosti Island. The men watched too, delighted at the smell of land and thinking of the food a landsman gets to eat. Surely there could be an end to eggs. Fifty years of eggs is fifty years too many; that's what they were thinking.

At Tadoussac a swarm of slim white whales came porpoising out of the Saguenay River into the St. Lawrence. On a height of land above the river stood the old resort hotel. A knot of bakers' wives watched the whales from a verandah. Inside, the bakers themselves, gathered for their annual convention, flailed about in a sea of Quebec burgundy. Things had gone pretty much to hell by the time the battleship appeared beyond the lawn.

"God, she's a beauty," sighed Bob Knodler, stumbling out to the cold grass. "German workmanship," he added.

"For Christ's sake, Knodler," snorted Ned Kitts, "she's a wreck." He held a wine glass in one hand. With the other he buttoned his blazer against the cold. "A freaking wreck. It's on the radio."

Knodler spent a few minutes groping in his brain for a reply. "Sunk your *Hood* with the first salvo."

Kitts bit the inside of his cheek. Anger deployed a pair of clown-like, bright red blotches on either side of his nose. His feet were freezing, but he wouldn't shift from the puddle he'd blundered into; Knodler might notice. He finished his wine carefully, tugged the side pocket of Knodler's jacket open with a finger, and dropped the empty glass inside.

"Sorry about the banana bread," he drawled.

Knodler shrugged. "So you cut your price. Big deal."

"I cornered the market."

"You took a hell of a loss."

"Made it back in a quarter," Kitts produced a broad smile. "And if you think I undersold you on banana bread, wait till your customers get a load of my blueberry cheesecake." He directed his smile at Knodler, holding it for ten seconds. Knodler kept his eyes on the battleship.

"Fastest, toughest warship in the world when she was launched. It's why the Brits were so afraid."

"Banana bread," Kitts grinned, "cheesecake. Be lucky if you're in business in a year."

Later a body of helicopters racketed downriver and circled the ship. The whales fled in a troop, filling the air with girlish chirps. A seal dove beneath *Bismarck*'s canopy of trailing plants. Cameras leaned from the helicopters. Lenses raked the ship. A girl in a fleece-lined bomber jacket hung in the wind with a microphone and reported live to CNN. Her hair streamed as she crouched in the open hatch. You could see *Bismarck* behind her as the pilot did a tight turn above the ship. This scrutiny didn't last. The battleship's demeanor was too dejected for TV. Shots that zoomed in revealed the piteous way she ploughed upriver, the slick that stained her wake. The crewmen of *Bismarck* waved at the helicopters, and a few cameras picked them out on closeup. But the men's faces were too dirty, old, and cracked, their merriment too pitiful, or else they stared with too much yearning as they strained to catch a final glimpse of the fleeing whales, arching whitely and vanishing, arching and vanishing. So the choppers clattered off.

At Quebec City the mayor put on his chain to welcome *Bismarck*. He'd even got a band. Doña Teresa perched on her Andean crag and watched the mayor's face dissolve as the battleship drew abeam and he saw, beneath the flowers, the desperation of this ship that had climbed into Canada with her last few tons of oil.

"Send this fellow our compliments," she breathed, "and one of Wickel's omelettes."

The German consul came aboard. Tall and thin, grey gloves, grey hat, an ardent wish to discharge his duty and be gone. The diplomatic protocols were not so clear. It was all he could do to keep his eyes from filling with tears at the battleship's condition.

Bismarck's senior surviving officer, Fregattenkapitän von Prenzlau, saw this, and would have liked to tell the fellow he could go. Still, one couldn't, could one. They had their duty, each of them.

"I am to inform you," said the consul, tugging a message from an inside pocket, "that the British battle cruiser is advancing into the Gulf of St. Lawrence."

The Fregattenkapitän thanked him for this news.

"We are not in a condition of war with Great Britain," the consul added.

The Fregattenkapitän understood that this was so, and said as much, and then presented, in his courtly way, both Doña Teresa and Hans-Adam, the Prince zu Westerwald. Relieved to have something to do, the consul clicked his heels and made Hans-Adam a short, dry bow. Hans-Adam raised an eyebrow and tapped a fingernail against his teeth, and looked away. The consul managed to locate a small supply of formalisms, which he produced in sequence until he had no more. For as long as he could he endured the hot black gaze of Doña Teresa. When he felt his skin was about to smoke, he spoke an unhappy farewell at the deck, clamped his face shut and hurried off.

"A plate of eggs for that one too," muttered Doña Teresa.

That evening *Bismarck* weighed, sailed past Cape Diamond beneath the staring cannon of the citadel, and made her painful way upriver to Montreal.

By now the news had spread that the battleship was something of a mess. The supply of dignitaries dried up fast. Frankly, most of them hoped the thing would sink.

And then there was that business with the bakers, the blasted bakers.

On his way home from the convention, Ned Kitts, drunk again, detoured to Montreal, bought the whole stock of his firm's banana bread from a supermarket, and enticed some English patriots to help him bombard the German consulate. Bob Knodler heard about this, and a vanload of day-old strudel, faithful German strudel, found its way onto the plate glass windows of the British Airways office. By the time *Bismarck* reached Montreal, the streets below rue Notre-Dame were snarled with partisans. In the Place d'Armes a German flag broke from the statue of de Maisonneuve; an hour later the police had fled in a hail of banana bread and genuine apple strudel. This brought the TV helicopters back, but not for long. Cake, for Christ's sake: cake! How do you cover a story like that!?

The girl in the fleece-lined jacket went away, and so did all the rest, and no one cared that a band played gamely on *Bismarck*'s quarterdeck, guided through a mangled march by Musikmaat Schreier, who had white hair and gleaming boots – smartest boots in the ship.

Picture a sixty-story building laid on its side, shaped like a ship and armed with enormous guns. Her sides gaped with old holes. Rust everywhere, a township made of rust – orange in certain kinds of light, golden and red, a fabulously complicated German town made on the river Elbe, sent down the ways on St. Valentine's Day. Now infirm, wrapped in a stole of blooms, she limped away from Montreal.

The river narrowed. She made a few knots against the current, along channels that rubbed past farms. A smell of cattle came aboard, of wet fields and cattle-punctured mud. Sunshine glinted on tin-roofed silos, gladdening the men.

They reached the Thousand Islands. *Bismarck* came slowly through these spikes of rock. Every island wore a crown of pines. Wild turkeys panicked through the undergrowth as that city of rust drifted through their sky.

On the islands cottagers prepared for summer. Hammers rang

in the cold. Old red Wickel and his darling, Matrosenhauptgefreiter Lipp, stared into the smoke of barbecues, into the cries
of children, barking dogs, the homeliness of spring among island
cottages. Lipp smiled, an expression made of perfect wooden teeth
– teeth carved by Wickel and never painted. Lipp moved his jaw
and smiled again, and the smile produced a wettish, clicking sound.

"Those boys are homesick," Doña Teresa said to the Fregattenkapitän, who sat in his command chair and watched the tops
of trees go by. He shrugged, letting the ash from his cigarette fall
in his lap. Doña Teresa noticed this and it displeased her, and she
touched a finger to her locket, altering its position on the starched
front of her blouse by at least a hundredth of a centimetre.

"It is fine for you to adopt these poses," she informed him sul-
lenly. "Someone must be concerned about the welfare of the men,
and whether it is fitting for German fighting men to suffer an
eternity of eggs."

"Madame," said the Fregattenkapitän, and his left hand, with
the pink stone signet on its small finger, left its armrest and trav-
eled slowly up until it hung above his head, wrist bent and finger
pointing down. The Fregattenkapitän's hair lay on his head as
insubstantially as smoke. He now touched this hair with the tip
of his finger, first here, then there, as if to make certain it had
not blown off. Then the pink stone ring returned to the armrest,
where it struck a worn place with a "tick".

On shore a child wiggled her fingers, bewitched by the apple
trees aft of turret Dora, and the swing that swung there, and the
bench. Another child waved, and another. Lipp flung a package
to the shore. The children tore away the wrapping and began to
stuff brown pastry in their mouths.

"Those insipid tarts of Wickel's," snorted Doña Teresa, peering
from the bridge in plain disgust. "You will defend this. You care
nothing."

"I recall a summer," murmured the Fregattenkapitän from a pall of blue smoke. "I was with my mother. There were pine-trees such as these," he flopped his hand at an island. "We talked about Picasso, all that summer."

"Art," snapped Doña Teresa. It was another irritant, like the cookies.

"My mother," continued the Fregattenkapitän, "had opinions of the cubistic art which were not generous opinions." He awarded Doña Teresa the faintest glimmer of a smile. She sucked in her breath and gave him a frosty look.

"I suppose you are famous for your sunny ways," she bristled. She might have pursued this indictment had not Marinesignalgast Epp, scratching at one of his large blue ears, come in from the radio room with a fax. Someone wanted to come aboard. A documentary was proposed. This was the burden of the message. Doña Teresa listened impatiently, scowled at him. "CNN?"

Epp scratched his ears and gazed at his hands. "Madame," he whispered, embarrassed, as if he could not imagine how this message had come to be in his hands, or even why his hands should be fastened to the ends of his arms. "Madame, it is not TV. Radio."

Matrosenhauptgefreiter Lipp, his body sweet with the scent of morphine, gazed sadly as the children slid away. A boy in a brown sweater scooped a handful of pastry into his mouth and blinked at the old sailor. Lipp raised his hands and let them fall. *Bismarck* moved upriver, a ruined skyline against a thin blue sky. She took the channel between Howe Island and Wolfe Island and shaped her course for the open waters of Lake Ontario. From the battlements at Fort Henry they watched her pass, struck by the wretchedness of her condition, even though they'd seen it on TV. Here before them she looked braver, as if her blossoms had been pinned to her for valor.

The battleship listed to starboard. A plume of oily smoke crawled from her stack and slid away behind to settle on the water, driving off gulls that had gathered to investigate her wake. At her stern she wore a rag of ensign, a bit of red cloth stamped with a cross. The rest had rotted off or been torn by gunfire long ago.

Slowly, very slowly, the little stone city of Kingston drifted astern. Amherst Island fell away on the starboard quarter. *Bismarck* made a course to weather the cape of Prince Edward county. The orchards and fields of Ontario drifted upwards on a trick of light, and occupied the evening air as if cut free of earth. From the foretop a lookout watched the shore of New York state and the rising foothills of the Appalachians. The battleship went up the widening lake. Doña Teresa touched her locket, adjusting it minutely. Hans-Adam stood on the port wing, and tapped a fingernail against his teeth. Lipp felt pain returning, and sat on his bunk and tried to smile.

"You have the pain?" demanded Wickel. "You have the pain?" But Lipp would only shrug, and Wickel stamped away to nurse his sorrow out of sight.

Westward they wandered into night, a night that toppled down upon them from a great height, madly pink, rushing down with the eagerness of spring, collapsing into darker shades and darker again, until the dying battleship was the same color as advancing night, and vanished into it.

iv

"I'M CHANGING MY name," vowed Mimi Mackenzie, gusting into the office and collapsing in a chair. She parked her legs on her desk, destroying a stack of color-coded files. "Red Palango," she enunciated. "What do you think?"

"Watch the files, sugar plum," said Anne.

Slumped, stretched out, displayed, Mimi's tallness was a force deployed to support her large grey eyes, her husky voice, her beautiful wide mouth. "The hair will have to get red," she announced to the ceiling. "Not major red, a sort of auburn with attitude. Add lip gloss, and I'm there."

Anne pointed at a pile of shiny faxes beside the files. "What do you think of the latest stuff?"

"We have enough research on this ship thing. I'm just not sure it's a story for Red Palango."

"Maybe not," said Anne. "Red Palango would be doing the story of her own life, a life made horrible by the abuse of her adoptive father, but which she triumphed over by dyeing her hair and discovering her own deep love for Antoine, her therapist."

"Christ," said Mimi, "I don't think Red would fall for a guy named Antoine. If a guy like that came near her she would knife him, although she wouldn't judge him harshly. Red is a woman who is fair-minded to a fault."

Anne nodded. "It's why her grateful public will be glad she's decided to take a whack at this battleship, and all the crap it's stirring up."

"Red loathes the public. It's why she carries a knife and makes her home in a slum like radio."

"Red makes her home in radio because she can't get a job in TV."

"How come that slut in the bomber jacket gets to work for CNN?" wondered Mimi. "Red is a legend."

"That's the reason there, chum. Red's legend is that she never gets to work on time, and when she does get there, she junks the files."

Anne Smythe's biographer would have to put her down as forty-two: exactly ten years Mimi's senior. Smaller than Mimi, or tinier, with a surface like a polished figurine, Anne faced the world with mandarin aplomb. Hating the shortness of her fingers, she simply folded them from sight. The result of this constraint was a neat, rectangular fist that looked as if it belonged to some peculiarly feminine martial art.

Mimi ran her hand through her hair. "It makes me look like a slut, this haircut, doesn't it?"

"I thought that was the idea."

"But *too* slutty, I mean. You don't want it *too* slutty."

"God, I wish I had a bust like yours," sighed Anne.

"It's true," said Mimi absently, "you really can't go wrong with it."

Mimi went about in alternating costumes, exchanging jeans and lethal T-shirts for a more chaste disguise, according to tactics. She knew that clothes were armament, just as she knew her hawkish nose was not a disadvantage and that her mouth could freeze men solid at a twitch. But her hair — her hair was a disaster.

"They never get this right. You'd think Carlo had learned to cut by braille. Fifty bucks!"

"Stop shifting your hips, OK?" said Anne, seizing a pencil in her porcelain fist and poking among some papers. A pack of cigarettes revealed itself. Anne made a short, sad noise, tapped the pack twice, then flicked it toward herself with a dexterous movement of her pencil.

"You promised!" cried Mimi when she saw the cigarettes. "You said you were going to try acupuncture."

"It didn't work. It doesn't work with everyone." She bit the inside of her cheek and, at the same time, made a sideways movement of her jaw. It gave her face a lopsided grimace.

"That is so sexy, the way you do that," Mimi said.

Anne contemplated the cigarette pack, a smart design of black and silver. "These are Turkish."

"And that's healthier?"

Anne fished out a cigarette with her knuckles. "I just like it that they're so expensive."

Mimi returned her attention to her ragged hair, pushing her fingers indignantly through it. "I'm going to go back and get a crew cut."

"I thought you needed major hair for the Red Palango number."

Mimi bit her lip. "They're sexy, those crewcuts, and you don't look like a hooker." She crossed one foot over the other and watched Anne grapple with the oval cigarette, attempting to light it without displaying her fingers. She accomplished this task with a sort of elegance, so that an act of purely personal reticence acquired a subtle bravura, as if her modesty arose from sensuality.

"Hookers have those haircuts too," said Anne, contented.

"It's illegal to smoke in here," said Mimi. "There's a bylaw."

"There's always a bylaw. We work in this hole because we can ignore bylaws. Otherwise, who would put up with the linoleum?" Anne ran a knuckle along the oval bulge of her cigarette. "Darling?" She let a silence gather. "I just want to make one thing clear."

"Sounds menacing."

Anne tilted her head and tapped a manila file cover. "I'm not in a hurry for this story, but I want you to get it right."

Mimi flushed. "I don't get things right?"

Anne held up a finger, for an instant, then folded it from sight. "You get drawn aside. I sent you up to cover the ship coming into the river, and you jumped that baker."

"Come on: one *night*!"

"Now he's taking out full-page ads. So's that German. Their bakeries are financing factions."

"And that's my fault?"

"How do you end up with these dorks?"

Mimi shook her head and grabbed her hair. "I should be working in TV."

"You're too impulsive for TV. TV would have you strangled. They'd stuff your body in a dumpster. It's how they think."

"Yes," sighed Mimi, fetching a breath of air charged with the smell of Johnson's wax, of steam pipes, of the ramshackle old building and the decaying craft it sheltered.

Anne crossed her fists demurely in her lap and lowered her eyes to Mimi's chest. "Straighten your shirt, will you?"

Mimi plucked her faded denim shirt by its shoulder seams and tugged it forward so it hung more loosely at the front. "Your skin is perfect," she declared.

"Of course it's perfect," Anne replied. "I spend a hundred dollars a week on it." She examined her wrist. "This new stuff is loaded with glycolic acid. It exfoliates the skin."

"What does that mean, exactly?"

"How the hell would I know?" She took a drag, tilted her head, exhaled slowly. Through the smoke she studied Mimi's hair. "Don't change a thing. Bloody Carlo is a genius."

V

ON THE MORNING of 14th April *Bismarck* reached Toronto and anchored beyond the archipelago that separates the harbor from the lake. Veiled in a mist of petals, the battleship settled to her anchorage. At the same time (and much was made of this on CNN) a cloud of small grey coral-spotted butterflies with yellow-bordered wings – thousands of them, hundreds of thousands, millions – appeared on the water and advanced toward the city. This way and that they drifted. Hours later they swarmed over *Bismarck*, crossed the harbor, and entered the city like ecstatic gods. Instantly they lost themselves. Perplexed by shade they blundered onto windowpanes and clung, as long as they could, stirring their wings forlornly as their color faded into dust.

The German consul found it disgusting, that he must step through fallen butterflies to reach his car. This business of the battleship embarrassed the consul, a wide man with a wide, squashed face and only two years left in a disappointing career. Cabled by his colleague in Quebec, he knew what to expect. His heart crawled down inside his ribs as he mounted the gangway. He was boiling in his thick wool suit by the time the young prince ushered him onto the bridge.

"Herr von Prenzlau," the consul said, "you must haul down your flag."

The Fregattenkapitän received this remarkable news. He directed an imperturbable gaze across the consul's shoulder as the diplomat shifted from foot to foot and dragged an enormous handkerchief across his sweating face.

"*Bismarck* is not a German ship," the consul squeezed his hands together, pressing the handkerchief between them.

The Fregattenkapitän did not answer this assertion, allowing it instead to flop to the deck, where it died. The consul drew a breath and arranged his lips into a smile, a grovelling expression that had irritated diplomats on several continents.

"I mean, Herr von Prenzlau, not *officially* a German ship. The question of the sovereignty of a ship of war, Herr von Prenzlau, I mean, naturally. . . ." His voice trailed away into a thicket of self-consciousness, and promptly lost its way. The Fregattenkapitän let his pale eyes drift across the consul's face. The consul gathered that his interview had ended, and left in disgrace, shamed even by the snow of petals floating from the battleship into the pungent sump that oozed from her.

Mimi and Anne climbed down into a hired launch. The pilot looked about sixteen, and tried to smirk at Mimi. She stared at him until he blushed. He cast off, and they chugged out of harbor through the eastern gap.

A ragged flotilla of partisans, not quite organized, growled at each other and churned witlessly about. A Union Jack and a large new German flag fluttered above the muddled boats. Sometimes a piece of pastry would sail up – a great, tumbling wad of banana bread, or a slice of German-style apple strudel, specially hardened and flung like a frisbee.

The launch motored into a slick and approached the weeds around the ship. Mimi riffled through some faxes. Two pages blew away on the wind.

"Damn it," snapped Anne. She made a gesture with her fist. "You infuriate me when you do this. Read the research, all right?"

Mimi stared at her. Another sheet blew off and floated upward. Anne snatched the file and sat on it. After a silence, Mimi flicked her finger against the file. "I'm not sure why you felt you had to come along."

Anne snorted. "You'd have dumped all this research, angel. Right into the drink."

"My main concern is the present."

"Your main concern is your hair."

The boy nosed the boat in among the weeds. A pair of otters and a snake slid from sight into the morass. Only a troop of frogs remained, opalescent frogs the size of melons, drunk on butterflies and camped in the sunshine on a density of water-leaves, blinking their amber eyes at Anne and Mimi.

"What's that humming sound?" said Mimi. "It's not the frogs."

Anne smoothed her trousers absently and pursed her lips. "Bees," she pronounced, and they could see them now, the color of dark copper, a dwarf race that roamed the ship in drowsy regiments. Dizzy with oil fumes they clutched at blooms, and sometimes missed, and tumbled to the waiting frogs.

A gangway swung against *Bismarck*'s hull and the boy brought them clumsily against it. Hans-Adam peered down as Mimi unfolded her legs and stepped onto the gangway. A gentle sea rolled in and wrapped a film of oily water onto Mimi's legs. Matrosenhauptgefreiter Lipp, anguished at this indignity, raised his hands and let them fall. Oberartilleriemechaniker Wickel clamped his teeth. Mimi got herself up the slippery steps.

Hans-Adam stood at the head of the little party, an eyebrow arched and his chin raised. He tapped a fingernail against his teeth and examined Mimi down his straight, thin nose. Mimi stared back, surprised at the jaunty squirt of hair behind his head, at the red elastic band that held it, at his youth, at the fineness of his face. Hans-Adam thrust his hands behind his back, raised himself briefly on his toes, and wildly searched his brain for a suitable phrase.

"Mimi Mackenzie," said Mimi finally, thrusting her oil-stained hand at him and wishing she'd never heard the name of Carlo.

"Of course," replied Hans-Adam, paralyzed. Why didn't Wickel do something?

"My boss, Anne Smythe," said Mimi. Hans-Adam met this assertion with a gaze as bland as dough. The scent of Mimi's body intoxicated him. He remembered that his uniform was threadbare and that he hadn't cleaned his nails. The smell of soap and skin: it made him dizzy. Intensely aware of Mimi's breasts, he kept his eyes firmly on her left ear until he was certain he could speak with carelessness.

"And it's a visit, this?" Why didn't Wickel just shoot him!?

"Sure," gushed Mimi. "I mean, we're here to do a story."

"Story?" Hans-Adam repeated numbly.

"Yes, story," Anne pushed in. "We sent a fax."

Hans-Adam turned a languid gaze in Anne's direction. He could have wept, he was so grateful for the chance to turn away from Mimi. "CNN?"

"Radio," said Anne, "we're from radio."

Hans-Adam seized this opportunity to tap his fingernail against his teeth and send an eyebrow upwards. "Mostly we watch CNN."

"Mostly," said Anne, "so does everyone."

"Why do you want to do a story about us?"

"We don't get a lot of battleships," said Anne. "They're not a big part of our daily life."

"Or anyone else's," said Hans-Adam. "That's the idea of a battleship."

"Good point!" Mimi blurted. "I mean, when you look at it like that." Anne served her with a pitying look. Mimi swallowed. Hans-Adam tried to glance offhandedly at Mimi: his face ignited in a blush. Anne raised a tiny fist and restored a strand of hair to its place. Lipp, affected by the nearness of the women, raised his hands and clasped them, sighed, shook his head, allowed his eyes to fill with emotion, and finally dumped the whole of this abject performance at Anne's feet, along with his wooden teeth, which clattered to the deck. Wickel shot him a savage look and blew his cheeks out in reproof. Hans-Adam gripped his hands behind his back and straightened his arms, rocked forward on his toes and broke through into speech.

"You'd better come in, I guess," he said to Mimi's forehead, then bolted into the safe stench of bunker oil and steel, rust and flowers. He picked his way forward through the maze of *Bismarck*. They followed a hallway like a tunnel, emerged beside a crater open to the sky. Flowers gaped from the rubble-strewn slope and bees went sifting through the blossoms in a puzzled hum.

From the labyrinth of the ship came other sounds – a ravishing noise of swallows; a dulcet hooting where the wind played pipes; a booming groan, as if some minotaur was closeted nearby, riven with grief at his ugliness. Hans-Adam moved through this with a light tread. The women stumbled after. A lightbulb flared in the tight companionway, then died away, lit and extinguished by a spasm of the generators.

They popped through a hatch onto the boat deck. A mob of hens screamed, rushed into a clump of bushes, and subsided into mutinous grumbling. A cat with smoky fur and yellow eyes glared at Mimi, and rippled from sight. Hans-Adam led the final scramble upwards to the bridge. They reached it suddenly, stepping through a door.

Swallows and purple martins chased each other down the long, wide gallery. A lone cardinal had flown out from shore. He perched in a smashed window, clearly baffled, and wrung a demented aria from his breast. Grass poked from fissures in the steel. Matrosenhauptgefreiter Lipp examined a tomato, desperately ill, that clung for life support to a net of twine.

Hans-Adam shrugged. "Vegetables just aren't his thing." Wickel glared at the vine, clearly a threat to the honor of the German fleet.

"Fruit," said Mimi.

"Eh?" Hans-Adam looked alarmed, and forgot to tap his fingernail against his teeth, or rise on his toes, or anything.

"Tomatoes are fruit, not vegetables."

Doña Teresa coasted down the bridge. Dust would not have settled on her blouse. It smelled of starch and the close attention of irons. Against this boardlike front her locket glittered. Doña Teresa moved it sideways with a finger, then touched her hair. Her tight grey curls looked knitted out of steel wool. She wore a gash of orange lipstick, crookedly applied. "No visitors for decades," she declaimed, "and now they troop aboard in crowds." She snapped her mouth open and extracted a thin expression that twitched at her lips, failed to become a smile, and fled. Mimi held out her hand and smiled modestly.

"Red Palango," she pronounced. Hans-Adam's forehead wrinkled at this news.

Doña Teresa stood straight as a pipe, jerked up her chin, and yielded the bare parameters of her identity. "You will already have met the Prince zu Westerwald," she added, uttering Hans-Adam's title in the manner of a criminal indictment, a charge that encompassed not only the bringing of these aliens to the bridge, but also his wretched uniform, his hair, that maddening tapping of his teeth. She pushed her locket a full ten-thousandth of a millimetre to the left and lifted her eyes reluctantly to Mimi.

"No doubt we must welcome you," she observed, and led them to the Fregattenkapitän.

Enthroned in his sea chair, *Bismarck*'s captain threaded the introductions faultlessly. He held his cigarette in his right hand, between forefinger and thumb, like a dart he was too tired to throw. An inoffensive pile of ash lay on the deck beside his chair. He bent his head at his guests and arranged his lips in a smile of exquisite courtesy. His skin was smooth and pallid. His pale brown eyes evoked a memory of warmth.

"You are a lady of the fourth estate," he said to Anne. "You are perhaps interested in the art?"

"The art?" repeated Anne.

"The art of your country — it is perhaps a vigorous art?" He dropped his gaze to his signet, which ticked against the armrest once. "My mother, alas, detested the cubistic art. I have retained a passion for this style." He raised his eyes to Anne. "If indeed it is a style at all, properly speaking."

"Properly speaking it is a load of nonsense," blazed Doña Teresa, "that is what it is."

A length of ash fell from the Fregattenkapitän's cigarette to his wrist, rolled off and fell to the deck. "Madame," he murmured in reproof, and raised his left hand until it hung by his wrist above his head, whereupon he extended the small finger, the one with the signet, and completed an inventory of his hair, touching one strand, then a second, finally a third.

Wickel had unearthed some decanters and returned to the bridge with a tray. His uniform looked as if a brush had strayed across it. Even his scowl seemed smarter. Behind came Lipp, his light brown smile clacking between his lips. They set out glasses on a chipped blue iron table that stood in an arbour drooping with yellow *Clematis rehderiana*. A company of bees staggered through the scented air. A few of them buzzed over to investigate when

Lipp unstoppered the decanter. He poured some liquid into a saucer and set it aside. The bees fell upon it, and Lipp got on with tipping measures into crystal thimbles, which he handed round. Doña Teresa allowed one to be pressed on her, and then another. Anne let her glass be topped up twice. She began to feel that possibly the old lady was not so awful, and the Fregattenkapitän might even be sweet. Mimi noticed that Hans-Adam's ears were particularly neat.

"You should let your hair grow even longer," she told him, adding his chin to a catalogue of perfect features.

"Of course," Hans-Adam dropped his eyes. Her arms astounded him.

"She called you 'Prince'," said Mimi.

Hans-Adam tightened his lips and arched an eyebrow. Wickel returned with a dented silver platter which supported a huge confection, rank with spirits. He set it down. It sagged, and threatened to subside entirely.

"Punschtorte!" cried Lipp. Wickel stepped back and glared at it. Lipp produced a knife. The Fregattenkapitän supplied a weary glance, Doña Teresa a blink of loathing.

"I know nothing about it," she breathed through her nose.

"It's in your honor," Hans-Adam announced to the deck at Mimi's feet. He could scarcely believe her ankles.

"It's dessert," Mimi confided to Hans-Adam, as if they were visitors together.

"I don't recommend it."

"We have to." She took a plate. "They made it for us."

Wickel flung a gauntlet look at Doña Teresa, seized a knife and pushed a quarter pound of rum-soaked sludge onto Mimi's thumb. "I still don't know your first name." She dipped a finger into the mushy torte and tasted it. Hans-Adam felt weak at the sight of her tongue.

"Of course," he gasped.

Wickel understood that approval was afoot. He troweled more torte onto a plate and thrust it at Anne, inserting it between her and the Fregattenkapitän, who was inviting Anne to agree that the cubists were not, after all, more arbitrary than, say, Caravaggio.

"Although their aims of course were different."

"Of courf," mumfed Anne through a mouthful of torte. The Fregattenkapitän received his own plate with a sigh and a length of grey ash.

"All this needs is a thickener," Mimi said, examining the beige mess.

"Thickener?"

"A commercial thickening agent." A silence greeted this surprising expertise. An arched eyebrow seemed the only possible response, and Hans-Adam supplied it. Mimi let her breath out. "I had a friend who owned a bakery," she confessed with a burning face.

"Ah," said Hans-Adam.

"I don't even know him any more."

"Our rule so far," Hans-Adam decided to reveal, "has been: no journalists."

"Have many tried?"

Hans-Adam scrutinized the torte. "No," he conceded, "none."

"Your English is terrific," Mimi told him.

"I watch too much TV."

And so things went. At first the bees behaved without reproach, devoting themselves to the orderly pillage of their saucer. A party of humming-birds tried a raid, and was repulsed. Later the bees became erratic. Mid-air collisions tumbled a score of fuzzy bodies into the saucer, where they drowned. The humming-birds returned and fed with impunity.

A breeze stirred the flowers. The Fregattenkapitän dozed off. Anne began to feel stifled, suddenly absurd, and the reception lost its way.

"Let's get out of here," said Anne.

Mimi looked at her, surprised. "No way. This has got to be the assignment of my life."

vi

THAT NIGHT, HOURS after Anne had left, Mimi lay awake in a cabin furnished with worn carpets and a bloated, dying chair. A chest of drawers tightened its lips and refused to speak. Against one wall stood a machine (it looked like a machine) of wood and brass, the size of a walk-in closet, its front pierced by a hole big enough to swallow an entire human, shoes and all.

On the bedside table Mimi had propped a photograph. She'd found it on the chest of drawers. It was a naval officer who looked like Hans-Adam, but wasn't.

A whack-whack-whack of blades advanced across the water as a TV helicopter clattered out and took some footage for the next day's news. Searchlights probed the battleship. Boats sped by outside, strewing the night with screams and the warring essences of fresh-baked goods.

Hans-Adam came and stood inside her door. Mimi made her breathing deep and watched him through slitted eyes. He stepped into the cabin. Mimi shut her eyes completely, afraid he'd see a gleam. When she looked again he'd gone, and the photograph was back in its original place. She slipped from bed, retrieved it, and propped it as before. Later she slept, lulled to sleep by the peeps of weasels as they roamed the ship assassinating mice and voles.

An hour past sunrise Lipp brought in a tray. He poured coffee into a china cup and removed a dome from a platter piled with scrambled eggs. A mauve bloom of clematis floated in a blue ceramic bowl. Lipp stood back, gazing with pride at his tray. He raised his cracked old hands and let them fall, swept his eyes at Mimi, fetched up a sigh of simple adoration and bobbed from the cabin. Hans-Adam popped his head around the door and presented Mimi with a demonstration of how perfectly a pair of eyebrows could be arched. Mimi regarded him from bed.

"Why not come in?"

"Oh, I don't know," he said, and stepped in anyway. "I don't recommend the eggs."

"I'm starved," said Mimi. She popped a forkful into her mouth.

"Wickel made them. They'll taste of curry. He thinks that goes with eggs."

"Yum."

Hans-Adam nonchalantly plucked the photograph by a corner and restored it to the chest. He adjusted the lamp on the bedside table. Then he tapped his fingernail against his teeth. Mimi noticed he hadn't shaved. Suddenly he picked up her coffee and drank it down. "Sorry," he said, although he looked more satisfied than sorry. He poured another cupful and put it in her hand, a contact that made Mimi blush. His beard looked rough. His teeth were very white. He stood quite straight. She saw him noticing her scrutiny.

"You were up last night."

He shrugged. "Of course."

"I was surprised to see you," she said through a mouthful of scrambled eggs. They tasted of curry, yes, and bunker oil too. Mimi gulped. "I mean, surprised to see you in my room." Hans-Adam's face remained unruffled, although it turned vermilion.

"'Cabin'," he said, "not 'room'."

"I'm not trying to embarrass you."

"Of course," he murmured to the deck.

And Mimi got around to asking him about himself. She had the upper hand, questions being her trade. To Hans-Adam the interrogative form was as alien as Mimi herself. Never exposed to such a virus, he stood there helplessly while Mimi emptied him of data. This is how she came to learn so quickly that his family had held estates at Westerwald for seven hundred years. An ancestor had been Pfalzgraf, a prince so powerful the emperor sent a daughter to him. A portrait of this princess had hung in his mother's room at Westerwald. His mother always said it was like having a picture of Hans-Adam himself, same eyes, same nose, same ears.

"And your mother?" Mimi asked.

Hans-Adam spent a moment memorizing carpet patterns. "Well," he said at last, "she's dead."

"And your father?" Hans-Adam pursed his lips and clasped his hands behind his back. He unclasped his hands and looked at her, then rapped a knuckle on the strange machine.

"He made this."

Mimi drank down a coffee, the way Hans-Adam had, in a single gulp. She viewed the machine. "What is it, though?"

Hans-Adam's hands resumed their place behind his back. "Possibly a toy."

"A toy?"

"Could be."

"You're not sure?"

"I believe it's a toy."

"How does it work, then?"

Hans-Adam tipped his head at the machine and shoved his hands in his tunic pockets. "It's broken, but I think you just crawl in the opening."

"Then what?"

"I think you lie down on that stretcher thing inside, shakes you."

Mimi poured herself another coffee. Her face acquired a satisfied expression. "You think, but you don't know?" She blinked at him. "Is that it?" Hans-Adam acquainted himself with Mimi's expression, then extracted the cup from her hand with a marvelous manoeuvre, drank the coffee, handed back the cup.

"Yes," he said, "that's it. I think, but I don't know."

Mimi looked into the coffee pot. Empty. She let the lid fall shut. "What would be the point of a machine that just shakes you?"

"Possibly it has no point."

"Toys have to have a point. They're supposed to teach you *some*thing."

"Well," Hans-Adam shrugged, "it could teach you to have fun."

"It would be fun to crawl into a machine?" A register of pique inflected this. She'd wanted that last cup. "It's fun to get shaken?"

Hans-Adam sighted her along his nose. "So my father apparently believed."

Mimi folded her hands on the blanket. "And you're a real prince?"

"Of course."

"I'm strictly middle class."

Hans-Adam accepted this information with a smooth countenance. He turned to the toy. "There's a lake at Westerwald, and by the shore he had another thing like this. In a sort of shed. I remember people laughing when he showed it to them."

"He probably was a lot of fun to be with," said Mimi.

"Nothing concerned him in the slightest."

"He had a lot of friends?"

"He had no friends at all, but people liked him, and he was famous, I guess, for his machines."

"There were others?"

"One would waddle into the water like a duck. It made a quacking noise, and swam quite well."

"And you're like him?"

"No one would be like him any more."

Mimi fanned her fingers on the blanket and studied them. "Is that why you didn't stay in your home, because you couldn't take his place?"

Hans-Adam tilted his chin. "Well, his place was here too, and I am taking it." He stepped away. "If you're staying another night, Lipp will get you anything you need."

"Your cabin," Mimi blurted, "you can use it any time you want." He paused in the door, his face averted. "I mean," she groped, "I know it's a big boat, but there might not be that many great places to move into."

"'Ship'," Hans-Adam said, his ears coloring, "not 'boat'."

"I didn't mean move in with *me*," said Mimi quietly.

"Lunch is at one," he said, and left.

vii

A NNE SENT OUT a package – clothes, laptop, mini-fax, phone. Mimi stripped off her oily jeans and tossed them in a corner. Steam billowed from a small zinc bathroom where a ship's artificer had got hot water running in the taps. Mimi ducked in and closed the door. The bath was almost full. She climbed into the stubby metal tub, lay back with her feet propped high above the taps, snapped open her phone and dialed Anne.

"I think he likes me," she confided when Anne answered.

"Naturally. Men always collapse before a slutty hairdo. Slutty hair is the history of the West. Maybe you can work that into the documentary."

"Seriously. I think we hit it off."

"Well that's just great, Mimi."

Mimi tried to turn the faucet with her toes. "There's no need to be sarcastic."

"There's no *need* to turn your assignments into personal sagas in which every toss in the hay is supposed to rivet me with fascination."

"That's not fair, Anne."

Anne drew a breath. "I know it isn't. But I get tired of you, Mimi. You take a lot of energy."

Later Mimi dried herself. She wiped the steam from a mirror

and studied her body mistrustfully. In the cabin she slipped into a chaste white cotton dress, a costume of electric modesty. On the bridge Doña Teresa and Hans-Adam had already encamped at the chipped blue table. A litter of newspapers made its way from the table to the floor. Doña Teresa was entombed in some account of foreign parts. Hans-Adam browsed, his face a sonnet on the topic of indifference. Lipp approached, displayed his woody smile, and left behind a tray of sandwiches and a jug of ferocious coffee. Mimi gasped with pleasure, and poured some right away. A silence followed, pricked by rustling newsprint, the tread of birds, and a whistling noise that came from Doña Teresa's nose.

Silences didn't bother Mimi. She was used to them. She often met them in her work, deployed against her. She'd learned to meet such tactics with a look of speckless innocence. Someone would break in the end, not Mimi.

She selected a triangular sandwich, bit into it, identified the taste of Camembert and popped the whole thing down. Doña Teresa clicked her eyes at Mimi. Mimi simply took two more sandwiches (smallish sandwiches, they were) and sent them on their way. Hans-Adam and Doña Teresa woke to the possibility that their lunch would be devoured from under them. They began to make their way into the present, sprinkling their path with sighs. Mimi snagged another pair of sandwiches and scoffed them down. At this the curtain of reserve was ripped aside and a blizzard of hands attacked the tray.

Ten minutes later not a crumb remained, and Hans-Adam began to fidget with a newspaper. Mimi decided that enough was enough. She crossed her legs in a way that made Hans-Adam blink, and a muscle twitched in his jaw, and he might have dissolved in a heap right there if a massive tomcat, smoky grey, hadn't drifted in.

The cat stretched, and aimed a careful look at Doña Teresa.

She ignored him. He leaned against her ankles and sounded a subterranean purr. Doña Teresa tipped her head forward, appeared to contemplate the cat, then launched it suddenly across the deck with an amazing motion of her foot. The tom skidded into an astonished chicken.

"I am too fond of cats," Doña Teresa confessed. "They take advantage of me."

Hans-Adam seized this moment to bolt off into the refuge of the afternoon. Doña Teresa returned to the news. The cat flattened his ears and vanished with a hiss.

viii

MIMI LOADED A tape recorder and went out to gather background sound. More boats were out, circling beyond the weeds. British and German factions milled about in festive anarchy. Mimi wandered the decks, got lost, found her way back again. She smiled when she came into the cabin and saw a length of paper curling from the fax. Eagerly she tore it off. Her expression fell. It was from archives, not the expected note from Anne. Mimi scrunched the paper and flung it away. She dialed Anne.

"It's Red."

"Palango, you cow. Don't tell me, let me guess. You are to be Queen."

"Princess, you nitwit."

Anne paused. "Are you sniveling?"

"No," snurfed Mimi, "yes."

"Why?"

"Maybe I should just come back."

"It's up to you," Anne said through a sizzle of phone noise. "But listen, here's something you should know. There's been some fighting."

"Fighting?"

"Last night your pal Ned Kitts and his baker lads went down to that German club on Sherbourne Street and started a brawl."

"That's odd."

"Didn't you tell me he was some kind of nano-Brit?"

"The Legion of Monarchists."

"There was a clip of him on the news."

"He admitted starting a fight?"

"He made a speech about how the majority is being forced to buckle under to minorities."

"You mean, it's time the majority stood up for itself?"

"You've heard this reasoning before."

"Sure, but not violence."

"It started with cake."

Mimi heard shouting, and went to the porthole. The boats had begun to cut across each other's bows, missing by inches. "You're not mad at me for staying out here, are you?"

Anne made an exasperated sound. Mimi could hear her scrabbling among some papers, looking for a cigarette. "I am a little mad. It's just the way you seem to have a *mission* to flatten yourself against anyone who flares his nostrils at you. It's irritating."

A rumbling attracted Mimi's notice. The grey tom stood in the door, pressed against the side and watching her intently.

"That's a pretty strong reaction," Mimi said to Anne. "Maybe you should ask yourself *why* it irritates you."

"Don't be dense," snapped Anne. "You've been reading those stupid articles again."

"I just think you could be more self-aware."

"I'm hanging up now."

Mimi sat on the bed. The grey tom advanced into the room with his tail held high, and made a slow perambulation. Every now and then he paused and sniffed, or leaned his body lightly against a chair, and never ceased to supply a thrilling bass line to the songs of birds, to the noise of water lapping, to Mimi's own soft breathing.

"You're a bit of a guy, aren't you," Mimi said.

The tom moved on around the whole perimeter, unhurriedly, at ease with all that occupied his mind. From time to time, from here and there, he stopped to assess her carefully, until at last, afloat with savoir-faire, he stepped across and leaned against her legs.

Mimi reached down to pat him, and he fled.

That evening Mimi and Hans-Adam wandered aft of turret Dora and sat on a bench. Dragonflies patrolled the apple trees. The city sent its clamour out on a breeze. A score of boats buzzed by, shouting at each other and terrifying the seals. The opalescent frogs remained unmoved, blowing their drowsy tubas at the setting sun. Hans-Adam listened pensively, and Mimi too, and the useless guns of turret Dora goggled overboard.

"It must be lonely for you," said Mimi.

"Oh, no."

"But there wouldn't be anyone to talk to."

"Yes, there would. There is. There's the crew." He concentrated. "The Fregattenkapitän, sometimes."

"But what are your interests?" Unbalanced by the nearness of his profile, only interrogation offered safety.

"War," Hans-Adam answered. "It's our main interest."

"I meant other things. You know, what kinds of books do you read?"

Hans-Adam nodded. "Yes, well, why?"

"In a documentary it's important to develop a human picture. It's the details that do that."

"Sometimes we watch TV."

"The news?"

"Sometimes," he raised his chin. "We watched it today," he added, sounding dejected.

"You saw the report on that fighting?"

He nodded again. "What kind of picture would we make, if not a human picture?"

Mimi examined her tape recorder. She made no answer. The reels turned, spooling the silent record of her confusion. Hans-Adam sighed. "Lipp and Wickel read novels to each other. The Fregattenkapitän mostly thinks. Doña Teresa follows the news."

"She couldn't do that at sea, I guess."

"Yes. We have the radio. We've got a fax, TV. We've got the Reuter wire."

"But where would you get those things?"

"Well, it's not always easy."

"That would sure be true." A bat, maddened by dragonflies, came pelting in among the trees. "You know," said Mimi impulsively, "let's fix that darn machine!"

"Machine?"

"The big toy! Let's get it working!"

He looked at her. "You're somewhat strange."

"Couldn't we!?"

"We might."

She lowered her eyes. "It's not just me who's strange." And a silence fell, a space into which Mimi slid a smile, aiming it downwards at the winding sprockets. "I just wonder," she murmured, "how you got the idea for that pony tail."

He placed his index finger against his lips and watched a boat slap by beyond the weeds. In the failing light he could just make out their fists. "And I," he said, "just wonder how you came to be Red Palango."

ix

THOSE RESPONSIBLE FOR provisioning *Bismarck* fell upon the pantry of Toronto. There was so much! Their faces acquired a glaze of madness. Unhinged, they began to make up lists, arguing fiercely at night among themselves. A torrent of pineapples swept aboard, a river of dates and frozen pizza, a microwave, popcorn that could be cooked in microwaves, fat-free frozen yogurt, eight kilos of biscotti, Belgian chocolate, California strawberries, cognac, a ten-pound wheel of cheddar cheese, flatbread crackers perfect for eating with the cheese. Someone discovered an attractively priced wine from the Niagara Peninsula. They ordered a dozen cases. Every kind of tangerine was marched on board, and types of lettuce that the men had never seen. The cook discovered Chinese food, and soon a procession of brilliant cardboard buckets wound its way aboard, trailing intoxicating wisps.

No˙one ordered eggs.

Other departments of the ship were busy too. Marinesignalgast Epp bounced happily about, his large blue ears pausing over boxes that contained a new computer, modems, a fiendishly small satellite dish. *Bismarck*'s communications had lagged behind the state of the art. Epp meant to change this, and he did, and to these other purchases he added a topnotch fax, way better than the old one. It was over this that a message arrived for Hans-Adam from Mimi, marooned ashore by her failure to think up a reason to stay longer than she had.

— *I have this feeling that I hardly know you. Palango.*
— *Was that your mission? zu Westerwald.*

She tore the paper off and returned to her desk to read it. Her face flushed at the sight of his printed name, a name that represented perfectly his calm demeanor, his eyes, that chin!

Lipp returned from a nursery with a bush of purple Vyvyan Penell. He would train it up that trellis by the stack. The nurserymen carried it aboard, along with a stem or two of Comtesse de Bouchaud, a summer-blooming variety with satiny pink petals and creamy stamens. Lastly they lugged on several dozen flats of bedding plants. No one disputed the Matrosenhauptgefreiter's right to these. *Bismarck* was his Tuileries. Soon it blazed with marigolds. A score of planters drooped with electric-blue lobelia. The Fregattenkapitän observed all this, as he observed the daily stream of messages, Hans-Adam's confusion, how Epp was enlisted to repair the toy, Wickel to scrounge for parts, everyone except himself and Doña Teresa captured in the mad entail of spring.

"One thinks of the ballet," he said to her suddenly one day. "You had a passion of the ballet, was this not so?"

"How would I know what was so or not so?" Doña Teresa raged. Her eyes flashed. "What is to become of the boy! What does he know of toys? What does he know of faxing?"

He was learning. For God's sake, the lights! The sounds of the city! The smell of the paper that unrolled with Mimi's urgent messages, demands for information, pretexts, accusations, furious retractions! Hans-Adam's head was boiling with the complications of a love affair by fax.

— *Why haven't you invited me back? Palango.*
— *You are invited. zu Westerwald.*
— *Great! Now you're acting out of guilt!*
— *Guilty of what?*

Mimi decided to pull her forces off this hill, and try another.

— *Why didn't you tell me there was an English ship looking for you?*
— *It was no secret.*
— *But they want to kill you.*
— *Naturally.*

Mimi's campaign squeaked to a halt when the Fregattenkapitän asked for help with ballet tickets. By this time it was plain that the battle cruiser *Hood* was hauling herself upriver after them. Mimi found tickets anyway. The Fregattenkapitän glanced at a chart, listened to an account of his old enemy, how she'd slipped past Montreal and gained the lower islands. No matter: they would attend the ballet in any case. The Fregattenkapitän was starved for the ballet.

Light applause spattered the marble lobby as the German party came slowly through. Also there were hostile stares. An older gentleman elaborately turned his back. Hans-Adam stiffened. The Fregattenkapitän ignored the insult. A length of ash fell off his cigarette unnoticed, and he bent his head at a lady who murmured a phrase to him, her lips trembling as if she might cry. Mimi blushed from the emotion of the moment, and it became her, contrasting spectacularly with her white shoulders and long black dress.

"It's not too dumb, this gear?" she'd begged of Anne.

"It's perfect, my little glow-worm."

"I'm trying this new lipstick. They say you can go with redder reds at night. You blot up the excess lipstick and finish it off with a clear slick."

"I'll say."

"It's too much?"

"Honey, you could spray on car enamel. Who would notice with a dress like that?"

"Fifteen hundred bucks," Mimi had grimaced.

"In for a penny, in for a pound."

Von Prenzlau and the prince showed up in antiquated cutaways and shirtfronts starched like boards. Wickel had polished their dress shoes into glass. Doña Teresa's head was motionless, bonded to the top of her ancient gown with epoxy made of pride. They'd almost reached the entrance to the auditorium when Ned stumbled into their path. He glared at Mimi, his eyes glassy. A shock of hair hung over his forehead and bright red blotches flamed beside his nose. An odour of bananas clung to him.

"Hi, baby," he grinned idiotically. Hans-Adam went white.

"Go away," said Mimi. "You're drunk."

"Embarrassing you in front of your buddies?" He swung an arm wildly and struck the Fregattenkapitän on the chest. It might have been an accident. The old man staggered, and fell against Hans-Adam. The prince gasped, his face like chalk. He could do nothing but clasp the old man's body in his arms. People rushed to help.

"That's not fair," someone shouted at Ned. "He's old! They're guests, for crying out loud!"

Hands supported the Fregattenkapitän. Hans-Adam stepped away, shaking and searching for Ned's face in the press. He felt a grip on his arm, and turned to find von Prenzlau's eyes on his. The prince could not control the violent quaking of his body. The

Fregattenkapitän pulled him to his side, and leaned on his arm, and Hans-Adam had to obey. They entered the auditorium and went slowly down the aisle. They took their places and the curtain rose. The Fregattenkapitän sighed as the *Sylvia Pas de Deux* unwound on stage.

"Balanchine," he murmured sadly. Hans-Adam sat in his seat stock-still, not even raising his hand to brush away the tears of helplessness that stained his face.

Was it silly to invite the ballerinas back on board? Anyway, how wonderful to have so many youngsters giggling on the bridge! If Wickel wished to stamp about displaying his mountainous resentment, the Fregattenkapitän would take no notice. Damn it, Wickel had his way too much.

Matrosenhauptgefreiter Lipp smiled and nodded and bobbed about after the capering girls. He rubbed his palms and drew attention to a clump of Nelly Moser that grew in a certain splinter gash, and nowhere else. The dancers stayed until the Fregattenkapitän learned that *Hood* had passed through the last of the islands, left Kingston astern, and begun to ascend the lake.

Mimi and Hans-Adam said good-bye at dawn, under an apple tree. Hans-Adam's collar was open and the ends of his unknotted tie stirred in a little breeze. Mimi's annihilated dress betrayed an excursion into the interior of Hans-Adam's father's puzzling toy, an adventure made plausible by wine and night, but now reduced by day. The thrum of *Bismarck*'s only living steam turbine rose into their feet. A stinging smell of bunker oil infused the orchard, and the first bees of morning stumbled forth to find the sun.

"I don't see why you have to go with them," Mimi repeated. "You're not old." She stared miserably at her evening bag. "Maybe I don't understand. How could I, with a name like Red Palango?"

"The Palangos are an honorable line," Hans-
wretchedly.

"Are you just going to forget about the toy? You
it by yourself."

"I don't even know what's broken."

"I should really come with you," said Mimi hopelessly, "for
the story."

"It isn't clear where we're going."

"Because of the other ship?"

"It's not a question of fear!"

"I didn't say that."

He looked at the harbor, his face a mirror of confusion. "How
could you come? We are a battleship. It's not just parties and ballet."

"You don't seem to have a very good opinion of me."

"It would be a bad opinion, that you like parties?"

"That I'm not serious enough."

"Serious enough for what?"

"For *you!*"

Hans-Adam sank onto a bench. He put his elbows on his knees
and dropped his chin into his hands. "We're not so serious. My
father made a robot that would turn the pages of a magazine when
my mother read in bed. A tape recording said, 'Permit me, high-
ness,' and a rubber finger flipped the page. She loved that silly
machine."

Mimi tugged his tie from his collar and put it around her own
neck. "I could love a silly machine." She knotted the tie into a
drooping bow. "Hell, I could even love you."

"You would steal my clothing, tie by tie."

"That's the idea, baby."

Hans-Adam stared at a boat that went bucking by, showering
an antagonist with pastry. "It would be disastrous."

An hour later *Bismarck* weighed. A few dancers sprung about on the island boardwalk, throwing mad *fouettés* at the ship as she made a slow turn and left the anchorage. Mimi kept her back to the lake until she couldn't bear it, and turned to watch. Down by the bows and listing, *Bismarck* pointed herself south across the bottom of the lake. Bright green water plants trailed out behind. Seals and otters popped their heads through the slime. Pink and purple petals, blue and ivory, drifted down from the cliffsides of the ship. Wrapped in a cope of fumes and aimless blossoms, of hope and hopelessness, the warship sailed away.

X

ONE DAY THE barometer plunged. Birds rose up in the midst of Toronto, masses of birds — a sudden, terrified nimbus of eyes and beaks, a storm of feathers so dense it hid the pink buildings of the legislature. A curtain closed across the government of men. Squirrels rushed about in terror of the screaming birds. Darkness fell at midday. Clouds blanketed the city. Still the barometer fell, squeezing the breath from people's lungs. Dogs with bursting eardrums lay in gutters and howled. Then the pressure rose. The sky brightened. Later it filled with snow. Flakes as broad as china plates came coasting down the streets. Out of this appeared the battle cruiser *Hood*.

"I hate that ship," said Mimi.

"You don't have that luxury," Anne replied. "You're supposed to be a journalist. Objectivity."

"Please don't be pompous. It depresses me."

The same boy ferried them out in the same launch. He whistled and stole glances at Mimi's legs and frowned as he looked for a passage through the partisans. This raffish hoi polloi had split, cell-like, into roughly equal factions. That one was British and the other German was deceptive: their followers might be anything at all. Like hockey fans from cities with no team, they had adopted someone else's. Many were young and unemployed, a naturally ardent class. Their latest fashion was body paint – red and white for British; for Germans, yellow and black. A thickening agent had been shaken into the air above Toronto, to immediate effect.

The strudel smelt of tar, and held together nicely when flung. And the banana bread, well, they made it with bananas, certainly; and rocks.

"What about the cops?" asked Anne, rooting in her purse for cigarettes. "It's getting rough out here. Have the cops said anything?"

Mimi shook her head. "They just don't want to know that this exists."

Anne found her pack, took out a cigarette and held it in her knuckles. She didn't light it, but stared at it suspiciously. A smell of seaweed rose around them as they neared the battle cruiser. Finally Anne crumpled the cigarette and dropped it overboard. "What about these pants?" she asked. "I should never have bought them. Nobody wears pants."

"They're perfect," Mimi stated. "You know that anyway. You paid three hundred dollars for them."

"I know what you mean about hating these ships."

"I meant *this* ship."

Anne nodded vaguely. "Frankly, I wish I had tits like yours. I hope you know how lucky you are."

"Sure, but this *hair*," growled Mimi. "That god-damn Carlo is trying to turn me into a candle."

Anne shook her head. "Uh-uh. Keep the wax. That wax is major Palango."

Mimi stroked Anne's head. "What about this? It's that new treatment, right?"

"It's supposed to re-structure the cuticles. It actually infuses the hair with vitamins." A Union Jack unfurled near them with a

CRACK. Anne yanked open her purse and shoved her hand inside, then pulled it out angrily and snapped the purse shut. "I feel so upside down! This *bloody* story. How come I'm upset and you're not?"

"I cried all night."

"Really?"

"I don't know what to do."

"I thought you were made of sterner stuff, Palango."

"No you didn't." Mimi looked at her. "Sometimes I think you send in Palango just to watch her fall apart."

"That slut Palango," murmured Anne. "She's made a mockery of all that is noble in the journalist *qua* journalist, and in journalism itself."

Mimi nodded. "Many say this, but Palango herself believes her bright flame burns in pursuit of understanding. It's for all mankind that Palango acts as she acts."

"Balls," said Anne.

"Another subject altogether."

xi

L IKE HER ENEMY, *Hood* slumped in the water. She dragged
at her waterline a whole sargasso of slime and sea-plants,
appallingly green. Narrow, weed-draped heads poked out of this
and blinked at Anne and Mimi.

A greenhouse rose from the after-deck. Here and there, in
patches of sun, elderly seamen puttered with hoses. Others hung
against the side in bosun's chairs and scraped at rust, sending it
into the water in a futile rain.

The officer who waited at the entry port had brown eyes, and
a cut where he'd shaved too close. His lips curved into the kind
of thin smile that sends cats hissing from a room. "Paget," he
announced.

"Anne Smythe," said Anne. "You're English?"

"We're a British ship, Smythe, yes."

"We're doing a story," Anne said, too loudly. Paget regarded
her tranquilly. Mimi gave her a curious look. Anne's face took
on a reddish tint. "About this war thing," she blurted.

"I should imagine von Prenzlau was useful to you, then."

"Red Palango," said Mimi, putting out a hand. Paget ignored
it. "It's interesting," persisted Mimi, "that you have spies."

This earned her a glance. "Spies?" Paget rested his brown eyes
on her forehead. "Sounds rather devious."

"Exactly," Mimi said.

Paget scraped out his little smile. "You are too kind." A liver-and-white spaniel stuck its head forward and sniffed carefully at Mimi's shoes. It raised a bankrupt countenance and emitted a despondent growl. "Be quiet, Wendy," said Paget. "She is not used to visitors," he explained, and touched a finger to the razor cut. He examined his fingertip. No blood. "Very nice," he observed.

"We're not anybody's friend," said Mimi forcefully. "We're journalists."

Paget rubbed vigorously at his chin. This caused the cut to open and his fingers came away with blood. "Damn," he sighed, studying his hand, and he led them to the bridge.

Hood's captain sagged in his sea-chair, sleeping, his fingers laced together on his stomach. He wore the remnants of a cardigan. Thickets of white hair grew around his ears. His head sprouted a silvery jungle that looked as if a hurricane had only just blown through. He woke with a start and peered through his woolly eyebrows at Anne. His eyes glittered like bits of polished coal, and when staring fixedly, as now, they gave his face a shrewd expression.

"These are our visitors, Sir Robert," Paget said.

"Solicitors?"

"They are here to spy on us, sir," Paget added pleasantly.

"These are the German ladies, then," he trumpeted, turning a black eye on Anne. He extended an index finger and jabbed it at her in a satisfied way. "Your countrymen flee before us, ma'am. I suppose you will not deny it?" He fetched an enormous sigh that swept the bridge with brandy fumes. A pair of Ring-billed Gulls raised a scream of protest and drifted off to warn their brothers. Their place was taken by a robin-sized bird, white and black, which hovered at the railing with rapid wing beats, and did not land, but uttered a high-pitched call and dove away.

"Least Tern," said Paget.

"*Sterna antillarum*," Sir Robert shook his head. "Not this far inland, no."

"Occasionally this far inland," Paget insisted. "No other tern would be as small."

"White forehead?"

"No doubt at all. Black-tipped bill."

"Ah, well, that's good, then," said Sir Robert. He turned his attention to Mimi. "It is Lipp," he raised a finger, "who has become unfettered in the matter of the clematis. Still," the finger waggled, "von Prenzlau could have stopped it." Clearly the clematis had been a grievous blow to German naval warfare.

"We're not German," said Mimi.

"A fine seaman, your Bosch," the old man confessed to Anne. His whiskers floated outward from the side of his head, like seaweed riding waves. "A fine seaman, but I suppose you will not deny it."

"What I deny," said Anne, "is being German."

Sir Robert examined his fingers unhappily, as if Anne's claim to not being German had drawn his attention to the condition of his nails, and it saddened him to see how black they were.

A short, thick woman bustled onto the bridge with a tray. Her hair was blonde, impossibly blonde, and lustrous to an unlikely degree. Her hands were scrubbed, her freckles polished one by one. She wore an immaculate apron festooned with sugar tongs and stitched with pockets full of shiny spoons that jingled as she set her tray at Sir Robert's elbow.

"Brought the tea, then, has she, Crickington?" Sir Robert said, addressing a tall officer who was leaning on a golf club, scowling.

"And the sandwiches," the lady addressed Sir Robert. "There's sandwiches."

"Thank you, Mrs. Wilcox," Paget said.

"He never eats the cucumber," Mrs. Wilcox said. "There's only a bit of chicken left. I'm saving it."

"They hide the chicken, Guns," Sir Robert told Paget.

"It's not fair," Mrs. Wilcox planted her feet. "I try to give him a bit of this and a bit of that. It's dietary."

"Thank you, Mrs. Wilcox."

"He feeds them sandwiches to the dog," Mrs. Wilcox said to Anne. "Over the side with it, I say, and generally I like a dog." This said, she left. Crickington put his golf club down and handed Sir Robert a cup. Anne caught a whiff of brandy. Sir Robert sipped, closed his eyes and leaned his head in Paget's direction.

"That's a whacking fine lass you've got there, my boy."

"They are our visitors, sir," said Paget firmly.

Sir Robert may have comprehended this assertion, or he may not. No way to tell. In the end he opened his black eyes and examined Mimi. "They have masses of chickens in the German ship. I suppose you will not deny it?"

"They have some."

"They are *stuffed* with fowl," Sir Robert pounded his chair. Mimi giggled – it popped out of her in a nervous spasm. Sir Robert looked at her with interest. "You're a whacking great lass, my girl." He emptied a cup of brandy barely compromised by tea, and put the cup back on the tray. He peered at Mimi. "We intend to kill your friends, but I suppose you know it."

Mimi stared. "Why?"

Sir Robert blew out his breath. Wendy sniffed, looked at Sir Robert, made a noise like "bluff," and moved off a yard.

"Guns," Sir Robert called, "why must we kill those chaps?"

"They are our enemy, sir."

"Exactly!" sang Sir Robert, returning his eyes to Mimi and pounding his fist again. "One's enemies, what?" He waved his curled fist. "They dine like *rajah*s."

Mimi's eyes filled with tears. She fumbled for her notebook, opened it, couldn't find a pen. She looked imploringly at Anne. The notebook fell to the deck. Wendy seized it.

"Give me that!" sobbed Mimi. The spaniel averted its eyes and took a firmer grip.

"Here," Sir Robert murmured, "you musn't cry."

"I'm not crying!"

He fished a square yard of linen from his sleeve. "Wipe your face anyway." Mimi blew her nose. A silence fell. A zephyr blew in, smelling of water. *Hood* shuddered at a tremor of her engines. Sir Robert sighed. "Give the child her secret papers, Wendy." The dog gave him a reproachful look, dropped the notebook, and collapsed to the deck with every indication of disgust.

"They're not secret," Mimi mumbled. She wiped the dog's saliva from the cardboard cover and dropped the handkerchief in Sir Robert's lap. "You're a bit of a bastard, aren't you?" she struggled to master her voice. Sir Robert heaved another brandied sigh and peered at the spaniel.

"I will not deny it, Wendy."

xii

"YOU'RE GETTING HIM an electric razor?" demanded Mimi two days later, lifting a list from Anne's desk.

"He cuts himself."

"And shirts?" Mimi replaced the list. "You know about men's shirts?"

"In fact I do." Anne retrieved the list. "You think they're covered by the Official Secrets Act?" She made a notation, her knuckles guiding the pen in a careful scrawl. The sight of this made Mimi suddenly resentful.

"And you think he likes you?"

"I asked for his shirt size," murmured Anne, "he gave me his shirt size. Period."

"A story that will set the world on fire."

Anne put down her pen and tilted her head. When she turned to face Mimi, her eyes were steady and bright. "Listen, dew-drop, the way I see it, your big claim to authority in the matter of the human heart has sailed away without a forwarding address. You think you have some advice for me?"

Mimi shrugged. "I thought you valued your independence."

Anne turned back to her list. "Bullshit."

Mimi lay her cheek on her desk and stretched her arms out,

letting her hands hang over the edge. "I'm so middle class," she moaned. "It's no good trying to hide it."

"You were trying to hide it?"

"I can't put anything about that toy in my story," Mimi changed tack. "It would expose him to ridicule."

Anne stopped. "Excuse me, we're not going to expose these guys to ridicule?"

"No one would understand."

"What's not to understand? They are ridiculous. We plan to ridicule them. Period."

"What about you and that Paget guy?"

"Ridicule him too. Just because he's cute doesn't mean I won't sell his ass to CNN."

Mimi sat up. "CNN? Who said anything about CNN?"

Anne folded the list and put it in her purse, snapping the catch with a competent procedure of her knuckles. "I just said I'd keep an eye on the story."

"You're *stringing* for CNN?" Mimi let her mouth hang open in a pantomime of astonishment. "That's a betrayal of *me!*"

Anne tapped a knuckle on the desk. "Tell you what, peach fuzz: I won't make you put in Lord Fingernail's toy if you won't make me pretend this job involves a principle higher than the piranha's."

"Well that really takes the cake, Anne! That *really* takes the cake."

Anne grinned. "Can't stay mad, can you?"

Mimi sagged forward onto her desk again, leaning her fore-head on the blotter and stretching out her arms. "How much are they paying you?"

"None of your business."

"It is if you're feeding them my stuff."

"Make you a deal: get that Palango tart back on the story. If she gets anything good, I'll cut her in."

"Palango is unmatched in the world of contemporary journalism," Mimi said to the blotter. "No speck of mud so small that la Palango cannot sling it." She raised her head. "It's her personal life that's a swamp of confusion. She thinks she can solve everything by leaping into bed."

"That's where she's right."

Mimi sprang up and paced across the room. "I don't know," she confessed to the evening traffic. "I think on a fundamental level he trusts me."

Anne nodded. "Right. So gut him."

"Well, I guess the truth can't hurt in the end."

"Don't be thick. The truth always hurts. That's why I'm using this new foundation." She stroked her cheek. "It's called starsmoke. It's supposed to add iridescence to your skin."

Mimi tilted her head. "It's perfect with that green."

"You really think so? I think I look like a leprechaun."

"You look like the Empress of Russia disguised as a leprechaun." Mimi sat down heavily and banged her feet onto the desk. "Look at us," she ran her fingers through her hair. "You'd think we were going out on our first dates."

Anne seized a pencil that had gone astray and aligned it parallel to the edge of her desk, perfectly parallel. "That guy is whacko for you, the prince." She opened a drawer and pulled out a pack of cheroots. Mimi watched her.

"What happened to those Balkan things?"

Anne slid out a pencil-thin cigar and lit it. "I thought I'd try these." A speculative expression formed itself around the act of smoking. "Revolting, aren't they?"

A postcard came for Mimi. "Entered canal 1600 hours," he'd written. "Down by bows one more degree. Buying pumps. Buying wiring for toy. zu Westerwald."

It was one of those cards with a blank front for the sender to draw his own picture. Hans-Adam had sketched the toy. Beside it he'd put an idiotic figure in a naval uniform, grinning crookedly. Mimi lay the card flat on her desk. She put her nose right against it and breathed the smell of ink and cardboard. She flipped it over and read it again. Finally she held the postcard close to her face, interrogating it, as if she might descry some further message in the picture of that silly, grinning figure, of the huge toy, of the hole that occupied the centre, and owned it.

xiii

MIMI'S TACTICS WITH a story were these: she liked to cruise out onto the savannah, slump in the grass like a lioness, and wait for the game to wander close enough to simply rake it in with her claws. Hating the long, hard stalk of research, she relied instead on bursts of savage interviewing. This produced documentaries with moments of illumination, and when narrated by Mimi herself, a slapdash charisma. Anne admired this, and distrusted it too. She'd supply research: Mimi would slink away.

"I didn't order you to include it," Anne said two days later. "I want you to read it, though."

"It was horrible, what they were involved in."

"Of course it was horrible. It was war."

"It's all archives. Archives, archives, *ar*chives. It's ancient history."

"The Punic Wars are ancient history. World War II is yesterday. It's still being fought." She closed a file carefully and flagged it with a red tab. Mimi pulled a stack of files from Anne's desk to hers. Red tabs meant urgent. Blue tabs, background on *Hood*; grey, on *Bismarck*. Recent news features went in the red files. Mimi jabbed her finger at a folder.

"What is it about you and files?"

Anne tapped a knuckle on a cardboard folder. "What I can't

stand about you, Mimi, is this terror of facts. This thing is dangerous. I want you to see that."

"If you really think this is a war, what are you getting involved with that English guy for?"

"I'm getting in*volved*," Anne raised a file and slammed it down, "because I am. That's all." She glared at Mimi. "God, you have a knack for irritating me." Mimi said nothing. "I guess you're going to tell me what's wrong with my life, are you? There's something sacred about you and whatever happens to you, is that it? You have some special insight that I don't have?"

"I didn't say that."

"You don't have to! You just parade around as if you're the *artiste* and I'm the drone who should be honored to help get your precious creations to air."

"I *work* at what I do!"

Anne retrieved a file from Mimi's desk, slid a loose page into it, tossed it back. "Like hell you do." She clipped a tab onto another file. "You take things as they fall in your lap."

Mimi got up and stood at the window. Traffic straggled up Jarvis Street. A filing cabinet slid open behind her, then shut. A stoplight changed at the corner; Mimi waited till it changed again.

"I didn't know you thought I was so trivial. Is it because of CNN?"

"That's it. You know us TV sluts. If it ain't on 'Larry King Live', screw it."

"I thought you supported my work."

"Oh, Mimi," Anne said tiredly. "See what I mean? 'Support' your work! You think everything you do plays itself out in a golden haze of passion. I'm supposed to stay back in the pasture, filing." She opened a drawer and searched inside.

"Why don't you invent a colored tab for where your cigarettes are."

"Piss off."

"You think I resent you getting involved in the story? I don't resent it at all." Mimi watched Anne rummage hopelessly. "I just didn't know you were in love with the guy, that's all."

Anne abandoned her search and sank back in her chair. "You're exhausting, Mimi. I'm not anything with anybody. If the alarm rings, I get up, all right? End of story."

Mimi opened a drawer and took out Anne's cigarettes. "They're always in here. You never put them anywhere else."

"I know. It's Freudian or something."

Mimi watched her light the cigarette and inhale. "What happened to the cigars?" Anne shrugged. Mimi lowered her eyes. "He hasn't called me."

Anne blew out a cloud of smoke. "Why did I suspect we'd get back to the subject of you."

"I've tried and tried to get through."

"Maybe their phones are out."

Mimi bit the inside of her cheek. "They've got more gear on that ship than Bell Telephone." She made her fingers riffle through a file, then closed it carefully. "I looked up his family in a book."

"I thought you despised research."

"How could someone like that care for a girl with a crummy hairdo and big breasts?"

Anne laid her arms on her desk, as if to compare her fists. She allowed a second to elapse before she spoke. "You think he'd like something smaller in a breast?"

A long silence followed. Mimi fought an urge to giggle. She made herself sigh, which seemed to help. Then she took a deep breath. This turned out to be a mistake, and soon both women were hooting loudly enough to alarm a pair of cleaners who'd arrived for the midnight shift.

xiv

STILL NO CALL from *Bismarck*. Mimi nursed her anxiety in the editing studio. She sorted through the reels of tape. One by one she laced them onto an ancient Ampex, then settled a headset over her ears. Anne took to waiting until Mimi'd sagged into her work, then left to visit Paget. Mimi knew this. Anne knew she knew. But a convention had appeared quite swiftly and inserted rules between them. Anne left without a word, Mimi stayed bent above the spooling tape.

Anne grew accustomed to the battle cruiser.

"I say, Guns," Sir Robert bellowed, "a type of food seems to have arrived." He prodded a tray of sandwiches. "Possibly we are to eat it."

"Tell him it's the cucumber," Mrs. Wilcox said to Crickington, who swatted his four-iron at some clover.

"One would think a ship's goat might be killed from time to time," Sir Robert blared. "They are not sacred, surely."

"Killed one last week," Mrs. Wilcox stated firmly. "You might tell him that," she instructed Crickington.

"Why does he call you 'Guns'?" asked Anne.

"I am the gunnery officer," said Paget, directing his binoculars at a flock of ducks that came in low and skidded onto the water. "Mallards. Very smart, those green heads."

"We are *ruled* by the cucumber," Sir Robert boomed. "It appears, and we must bend our knee." He peeled back a slice of bread and sniffed, discerning nothing: his sense of smell had perished thirty years before when a virus had entered his nose and trashed the place.

"Nothing wrong with a cucumber," Mrs. Wilcox countered, snatching the bread from Sir Robert and slapping the sandwich back together. "It's ecological." She handed Sir Robert a cup that smelled like a tavern. Sir Robert slurped at it and made no more complaint. Mrs. Wilcox, trailed by Crickington, retreated to a cabin curtained with chintz and brightened by shelves of china. Mrs. Wilcox liked a bit of china. Crickington hated it, just as he hated her blasted python, a creature who'd slithered into *Hood* and found a paradise of rabbits.

"Thick as a tire, that bloody snake," carped Crickington.

"They're vermin, them rabbits," Mrs. Wilcox would reply, "that snake should get a medal." Then she'd haul out a massive tortoise-shell comb and rake it through Crickington's stringy hair. "It wants a bit of trimming, this."

Anne made a date with Paget. Damn it, he'd never do it himself. Just listen to him.

"Bonaparte's Gull," he was insisting to Sir Robert.

"*Larus philadelphia?*" Sir Robert shook his head. "I doubt it."

Anne marched straight into this exchange and yanked the binoculars from Paget's hands.

"Eight o'clock," she said, "on that beach over there."

"But, the beach, Smythe?"

"Just be there."

Cold sand filled her shoes. She tried to empty them, balancing on one leg, then the other. They filled as soon as she slipped them on again. She gave up and trudged down the beach carrying her shoes. Ghostly windsurfers in rubber suits slid onto the lightless water and shot away. Paget's cutter appeared as a wave among these vanishing sails, a wave that quickly grew a bow. He ran the cutter straight onto the beach.

They made their way to a gravel parking lot. Paget watched a rubber-suited windsurfer unload his board and stagger off into the sand. "Fun, is it, Smythe?"

"I don't see how it could be."

"And what about this?" Paget wondered as he wedged himself into the narrow bucket seat.

"You're just afraid I'm going to bite you," said Anne, putting the car in gear and tearing out of the lot, "and I am."

XV

THE HEADSET HUNG from Mimi's neck. She sorted through a stack of reels, interviews she'd done with *Bismarck*'s crew. She laced one onto the machine. Lipp's voice began a careful articulation of the ratio of compost, peat, sand and bonemeal favored by the genus *Clematis*. Mimi hit the rewind, snatched off the tape and tossed it aside. She made her way to the basement, fed a handful of quarters into some machines and returned to her stool with a chocolate bar, a coffee, a bag of chips. She tried to listen, feeding her concentration with successive bursts of sugar, caffeine, sodium. The sea had crawled with enemies, this much she understood. A fleet went out to look for *Bismarck* in the fog, but the Germans had eluded them, taking the passage west of Iceland. All this went into Mimi's ears, along with dreamy memories of Greenland sighted suddenly through lifting fog, a coast of mountains hacked from ice and sparkling in the sun. Later a pair of cruisers caught *Bismarck* in the Denmark Strait, and after that the fight, the chase, the long dismemberment by cannonade. It was too much for Mimi, who placed Hans-Adam into every scene. Why did they have to remember *every*thing? She tore the headset off and swung it against the editing machine. An earpiece broke off. She slammed out into the office and stalked down the hall to the newsroom. The night editor was sprinkling fish food into an aquarium.

"I don't see how anything can live on that sawdust!" Mimi fumed.

The editor wiggled his finger in the water. The fish drifted to the bottom of the tank. "It's the most expensive kind there is," he said, "but they die anyway. Maybe it's the light in here."

"What light?"

"That's what I mean." He had a lumpy face, fed by a diet of doughnuts and skepticism.

"I'm working on this *Bismarck* thing," said Mimi, peering at the quailing fish.

"You're scaring them."

"We think it's an important story."

He put away the box of fish food. "Great. I'll pull the guys off O.J. Simpson right away."

She sniffed at the tank. "It's this water. You should change it." She lifted a newscast from his desk, rustled through it. "Why are you ignoring the ships?"

"I'm not. Nobody is. We keep an eye on them."

"You think it's crazy." A goldfish with drooping fins forgot its fear and examined her against the glass. The editor emptied a coffee mug at the drinking fountain, filled the mug with water and dumped it into the tank. It added a turbid cast to the aquarium.

"You should have rinsed that," Mimi said.

The editor nodded and wiggled his finger at the surface. "They die anyway."

Later Mimi tried to call *Bismarck*, and failed again. "Oh, God," she wept. Tears of frustration, angry tears, stained her face. "Oh, baby."

Marinesignalgast Epp and Hans-Adam regarded the useless telephone with expressions respectively of impotence and reproach. *Bismarck* swung at her chains in Lake Erie. Number Two starboard boiler had taken to its bed. Oberartilleriemechaniker Wickel, whose sceptre waved over the entire ship, raged at Stabsober-maschinist Merz, at Maschinenmaat Nissel, at every one of that wretched crew who toiled with dwindling hope in the power plant. Wickel raged, but *Bismarck* had retired for the night, as had her phone.

"It is a question of the batteries," sighed Epp. "Without the power, they have lost the charge."

"It's junk," remarked Hans-Adam, rising onto his toes. His fingers were knotted behind him and he clenched his jaw. "Useless junk."

"Young women are at any rate quite busy with their lives," Doña Teresa observed from her private cloud of satisfaction. "I believe it is the modern way."

"Emergency batteries?" Hans-Adam asked Epp. "Backups?"

Epp dug a screwdriver into a blue ear and fetched a regretful sigh. Hans-Adam nodded.

"It's not your fault," he muttered, giving Epp to understand that, clearly, it was.

"Spilt milk," murmured Doña Teresa, and glided away to a heaven made of peaches.

Hans-Adam retreated to his cabin in despair. Lipp, in pain himself, hovered at Hans-Adam's door in a haze of narcotics and maternal worry. He bobbed his head at Hans-Adam, raised his hands and let them fall. Finally he drifted off to find Wickel. He made his request. Wickel promptly refused. Lipp did not argue, only dribbled a liquid look at Wickel's boots. Wickel gnashed his teeth and crumbled. He stamped away and bullied together enough hands to swing out the launch. Lipp returned to Hans-Adam's cabin with a compass and an oil-smudged chart. Hans-Adam took these, gave Lipp a searching look and kissed him tenderly.

With the city of Buffalo as a beacon, Hans-Adam found his way into the Niagara River. To his right lay the state of New York;

to his left, Ontario, and the lights of Fort Erie. He shot into the river and dashed downstream. He swept through the night, surging over murderous currents that heaved their shoulders at the surface. At last he could see the distant, floodlit glow of Niagara's plume. He heard the cataract's killing sound.

He ran swiftly in to shore and found a stubby quay with iron bollards. Soon he was running down a road that wound along the river and through a wood. Thousands of white trilliums glimmered among black trunks. He came out of this shoreside park, found a lighted building, found a phone.

"Oh, God," Mimi gasped when she heard his voice. "Oh, baby."

She drove from Toronto to Niagara Falls in one long hurtle around the top of Lake Ontario. She raced into the lobby of the Sheraton and found Hans-Adam panthering about between the sofas. They skidded to a halt and stared at each other while their chests heaved in and out and a sudden fog of bewilderment seeped upward from the floor. Hans-Adam straightened his arms and clasped his hands behind his back. He rose on his toes and examined the top of Mimi's head, frowning as he did.

"We better get a room," said Mimi, understanding that if she did not take over, no one would, and the whole night would crash to an end with the sound of a fingernail tapped against a tooth. "Don't worry about my hair," she took him by the hand, "I'm getting it cut."

xvi

"I GUESS YOU THINK I'm nuts, buying these," said Anne, as they loaded the last of the bedding plants into her car.

"Nothing wrong with it," he said. "A rite of spring, isn't it?"

"Last night was a rite of spring." She closed the trunk and paused with her fists on the lid. "Sorry. That was a stupid thing to say."

"You are too hard on yourself, Smythe," he got into the passenger seat and shut the door. He hadn't touched her since early morning, when she'd rolled against him and he'd seized her again. She started the car and headed for the lake. Why didn't he touch her? Was he embarrassed? Was it her stubby fingers folded into fists?

Paget carried a dozen flats from the parking lot to the cutter. There were pink snapdragons, tiny purple pansies, pansies with purple-and-yellow patterns like wolves' faces. Morning glories clung to little stakes. A bushy daisy occupied a terracotta pot.

"I feel silly," Anne confessed as they motored off.

"Yes," said Paget. They cleared a little headland and approached *Hood*. A smell of oil clotted the air, and rust. Oily bilge ran down the battle cruiser's side. The barnlike greenhouse glowed in the morning light. A water-serpent, heaped on some weeds, raised its narrow head.

A pair of tottering artificer's mates with suspiciously seraphic faces helped unload the flats. The air inside the greenhouse was thick and cloying. An army of cucumbers lay sloppily encamped, as if they had only paused for a mouthful of earth and would soon be slithering away. A race of malevolent beans glowered from poles and a species of tomato drooped, inconsolable, from the barrels of Y turret.

The place was empty except for a grimy giant on his knees among some beets. He waved away a fly. The gesture cast a rain of dirt onto some leaves. He caught sight of Anne and Paget, made a doleful noise and struggled to his feet. A brier pipe sagged from his mouth, sadly, as if both pipe and mouth had formed a friendship based on misery. A steady relay of insects investigated his cavernous ears, perhaps even lived inside. His eyes shone dully through a screen of eyebrow.

"What's this, Wrinch?" asked Paget as they lay their flats on the deck.

"Snaps," he replied, bending his face to examine the plants. He prodded a bloom. "Them little ones is pansies."

"Not the plants. What I meant was – why are you alone? Where are your mates?"

The old man shook his head. A drop of brown smoke oozed from the pipe and dribbled to his chin. He looked about the empty greenhouse. "It's a bad business, sir. Mrs. Wilcox's snake has took the last of the goats." Wrinch presented Paget with a face like a sacked city. "Sir Robert's in a right rage." Paget sighed. Wrinch knelt heavily. His fingers were as thick as winter carrots. He caressed a morning glory. "I'll put these in up top. They like a bit of light."

"Yes," said Paget.

Wrinch sniffed at a flat. He deposited a crumb of soil on his tongue. "Loamy," he judged at last.

"That's good, is it?" Paget sounded annoyed.

"There's them that says so," Wrinch confessed, as though this too were cause for grief.

Paget and Anne climbed into *Hood*, into a twilight soft with ferns. Tree-frogs chirped nearby. Things darted past their feet. Once Paget lost his way, pausing at a ladder that disappeared down a hole.

"I should never try these shortcuts."

Suddenly an old man thrust his head from a door. "It's Warrenhook again, sir! He's stolen my best mare!"

"That's all right, Billings," said Paget wearily. "You know he'll give her back."

"If you can't trust a chap you went to school with," the old man cried, ignoring Paget's reassurance, "who can you trust?" He hopped with rage.

"Very well," said Paget. "I'll send someone round to have a word with him."

"If you can't trust . . ."

"That's all, Billings," Paget snapped, and they turned away.

"There can't be horses," Anne prompted.

"It's turtles," Paget rubbed his eyes, "they race turtles."

By the time they reached the bridge Sir Robert had sealed himself behind a screen composed of gin and fury. He clutched a teacup, trembling. Mrs. Wilcox surveyed the tea things defiantly.

"Ah, Guns," Sir Robert shouted, his voice cracking under a fresh charge of anger.

"I know," said Paget.

"Shall I put out some sandwiches, sir?" said Mrs. Wilcox, addressing herself loudly to Paget. Sir Robert stared at her as if she'd waved a fistful of vipers at his nose.

"Crickington!" Paget snapped. Crickington beheaded a dandelion with a swish of his five-iron. He had a smile like a carving knife. "I spoke to you!" barked Paget. "Report, can't you?"

"Report?"

"You are master-at-arms?"

"It's not a job for an officer," Crickington replied, aggrieved.

"You are too grand for us, Mr. Crickington," scoffed Paget.

"I've sent a party out," Crickington muttered. "Anyway, they'll never find it."

"Stop swinging that club!"

Crickington shuffled into a more respectful bearing. "It's not my snake, sir," he said in an injured voice, shooting a glance at Mrs. Wilcox. "I've not caused the trouble."

Paget shook his head. "Just get on with it."

"When animals get swallowed, it's no pet of mine that's done the swallowing."

"Your escutcheon is unsullied, Crickington."

"When it's choking that gets done . . ."

But Paget had already left.

Paget's enormous cabin, once the admiral's, reflected the battle cruiser's old prestige. A marble mantelpiece, a pair of faded sofas, fabulously dusty Shiraz carpets. A cracked oar hung on a bulkhead – trophy of some old race.

On a desk, two photographs in leather frames. One showed a younger Paget in whites, squinting in sunshine at the camera. The other must be his parents. Anne picked it up. A large woman in a sleeveless frock held her arms awkwardly away from her body; a small man in a clergyman's collar could not conceal his embarrassment. Anne noticed Paget watching her.

"Sorry. It's the snooping gene. Can't help it."

Paget shrugged. "Not much of interest." He opened a small cabinet. "It'll have to be sherry."

Anne replaced the photograph. "It's still morning."

Paget poured a finger's width into each of two glasses, and put

Anne's on the desk. She left it there, her eyes attacted by a row of watercolors: birds and seascapes. They were bare and oddly fresh, and in that cabin looked like souvenirs of some impossibly vivid present. In one, a gull spread its white wings against a cruel sea, and opened its beak to release a cry made yet more plangent by its silence. The background was barely indicated, a few waves cresting, an effect of great distance, a distance that did not stop at any shore but continued past the rim of Earth.

"It's wonderful!"

"Oh, hardly," Paget said curtly.

"But they're yours!"

"I wish you wouldn't even look at them," he said. "They're only silly." He emptied his glass, picked up a printed list from his desk and sat on a sofa. Anne sat beside him and took the list from his hands.

"Why don't you look me in the eye? You hardly ever look at me."

Paget got up. "I am not polite enough. It's another thing that happens to us."

"Yes, you put it like that and you make it sound like an initiation into the warriors' locker room." Her knuckles neatly clamped the printed page. "It's like your mumbo-jumbo, you're proud of it."

Paget drummed his fingers on his chin. "Our way of speaking, do you mean? It's only jargon." He stopped drumming and examined his fingers. "It may be true that we enjoy confusing people."

"Do you think it's noble, all this?"

"God," said Paget, nettled. "What's that to do with it? It's simply that there exists a class of person known as enemies." He opened the cabinet, but shut it immediately, taking nothing out. "We are only an extension of you yourselves, Smythe, except with larger guns."

"Oh, very neat! Do they give you a little book with those answers?"

"No, we memorize them." He found a tablet on a table, tore off a heavy sheet and clipped it to an easel. He dipped a thin brush in a jar of water, and began to moisten a disk of color in a tin tray. Anne watched the quick, deft motions of the brush.

"I don't think you're being candid. You must find some romance in the idea of war."

"Nothing of the kind. It's my profession." He flicked the brush over the paper, and a sea took shape. The sea, a breaking wave, the outline of a gliding bird. Anne bit the inside of her cheek and forced her glance to the list in her hands. "It's odd," she said, running a knuckle down the typed lines, "that part of your job would be ordering biscuits."

"That's what women hate about the navy, that we take time to order pastry items when we're off to kill each other."

"Pastry items. You make it sound like ammunition."

"It's all rather ordinary, I'm afraid."

"Biscuits, hard, boxes five dozen," Anne read from the list. "Biscuits, soft filling, boxes five dozen."

"Biscuits," recited Paget by heart as a gull appeared beneath his brush, "chocolate thin wafer, boxes five dozen." Suddenly tired, Anne released her grip on the list and let it slip to her lap. Paget finished. He unclipped the sheet and handed it to Anne. "They're all I ever do, these views." This gull's beak was open in this one too, and the sea behind it limitless. "I only give it so you'll see it's just a silly trick."

"It's not a silly trick." She looked at Paget, but his eyes slid away. He picked up her neglected sherry and drank it down at once.

"Don't often do that," he frowned at the glass. "Look here," he said, drawing a breath, "I must tell you we shall weigh at dawn."

Anne sat staring at the paper in her lap, watercolor and printed list, postcards from the world of human needs, the world of water-colors, biscuits, turtle food. "You're right," she said, "I do hate it. It's too crazy for me. How can you fight when your world's so day-to-day?"

"There's always time."

Hood brought in her anchors at six o'clock next morning. Black smoke billowed from her funnel. She trailed oil. A stain of oil ran down her side from the forward starboard six-inch gun, which her gunners, seized by some optimism, had begun to lubricate.

No dancers kicked their legs at the battle cruiser, although a forest of British flags shivered on the Leslie Street landfill. She hauled herself round by inches onto a southerly course. A squadron of yachts put out to escort her. The smoke drove them off and they put back in.

Hood ran up her ensign. It broke to an onshore breeze. An aldis lamp blinked out a message from her bridge. "Farewell." The German consul read this through binoculars, and found his emotions hard to supervise. He put the binoculars away and wiped his eyes with his handkerchief.

"I give you the hunter's toast," he whispered.

Anne stood in the empty pavilion at Sunnyside, in the long grey rectangle of the upper promenade. She watched the warship take herself into the channel, spreading at her side that dazzling, viscous train of vegetation, of seals and otters, of lizards dizzy with oil and morning light.

xvii

MIMI AND HANS-ADAM clambered back on board just as *Bismarck* crawled away from Buffalo. The machinists had coaxed and bludgeoned Number Two starboard boiler until at last the thing had rubbed its tired eyes, hitched its suspenders, and spat on both its hands. The battleship went wobbling up the lake to Cleveland, bug-eyed with the effort, and that was as far as she would go. She lay there now, off the Ohio port, sunk in a coma. Stabsobermaschinist Merz and his mates took up their instruments and prepared to go at her again. Only Maschinenmaat Nissel would not assist in this: he was too drunk, and making impassioned speeches to his stamps. They did their best without him, battering hopefully at anything that looked as if it might be cudgeled into life.

Disturbed by hammering, drugged by fumes, bees droned out and fell in clusters to the opalescent frogs. Bats too, alarmed by the hammers, poured from crevices – a wind of frightened mice. They seethed into the daylight, milled about, found a new cave and poured back in.

Bismarck's needs were many: not only bunker oil but wine. That sweetish, cheapish wine from the Niagara Peninsula – they'd formed a taste for it. They'd finished all they'd bought. They longed for it now, and wandered about with mournful, wine-sticky mouths. Lipp was running low on morphine, so that was needed too, and he wanted a new type of pruning hook. Really, the orchard was pathetic, ravaged by salt, clinging to its hopeless raft of earth astern. But at least it smelled of apples, and people liked to sit there, and Wickel loved Lipp desperately. If Lipp wanted a pruning hook, why Lipp must have it.

The list of things to buy in Cleveland grew. Now it included seed potatoes. Red Pontiac, Lipp specified: a handsome, red-skinned type that would produce those tiny spuds that Wickel loved. Lipp thought they'd do well near the stack; they tolerated heat. He wanted Lady Fingers too, a pretty tuber, and no thicker than an inch.

"As candy," Lipp murmured from his bunk. "They are as candy."

"You have the pain," said Wickel furiously, studying Lipp's face. The skin was waxy, yellow.

"Make a trench for the potatoes," Lipp said tiredly. "Cut them, and place them with the cut side down."

"Place them yourself!"

"As the potatoes are growing," Lipp instructed, closing his eyes and thinking of the coolness of earth, "you must hill them. This means to pull the soil around them, keeping them covered as they grow."

"Dirt," growled Wickel.

"Earth," sighed Lipp, and slept. Wickel went off in a rage, stormed forward to berate a gun crew lolling near turret Bruno. Later he castigated a bosun's mate in charge of swinging out the launch. It's true the men were a little drunk, and one of them sound asleep, but certainly this would not have troubled the Fregattenkapitän, and it was he who'd ordered the launch.

The Fregattenkapitän had sailed into his declining years on a dream of ballerinas and of marble statues, a dream of boyhood journeys with his mother south to somnolent palazzos and villas slung from mountainsides. Later he'd discovered Picasso, and of course, the meaning of everything.

"Meaning of nothing," his mother had said.

"Charged with ruthlessness," he'd bragged, proud of this observation, which he'd read.

"Charged with nothing," his mother had replied, too sublime to brush away the tear from her eye.

Sailing away to war, the Fregattenkapitän had no idea what had happened on the picture plane since then. It was only when they'd lain off Buffalo and he'd slipped ashore to a museum, that the canvases of Rothko and Still had seemed to proclaim the end of all his world.

"He speaks of these things," said Wickel bitterly. "Why for?"

"He thinks of the art," insisted Lipp, soothed by an injection. "The art has been his life."

"The war!" hissed Wickel.

But Lipp could not be bullied. "Herr von Prenzlau," he maintained serenely, "has the happiness of the art."

But Herr von Prenzlau had no such thing. He had the confusion of the art. The great, dreaming canvases of Rothko and the howling universe of Still – who could he ask about them?

"They disturb me," he admitted to his long-dead mother, addressing her out loud.

"Charged with nothing," she persevered.

"I cannot agree," the old man murmured on the bridge.

These colloquies offended Wickel. Against them he could oppose nothing but his grief, his memory of Lipp as a youth with a smile that could melt bones. He struggled against the Fregattenkapitän's implacable remoteness. He struggled against Doña Teresa. He struggled against this madness of the prince, a madness that had forced the Oberartilleriemechaniker to waste time and men carting that foolish piece of junk from the prince's cabin to an open spot on the deck near turret Bruno. Wickel struggled against this, and got nowhere. In retaliation he had nothing to wield except a rusty sabre of vituperation swung downwards at the crew.

"You know," said Mimi as they descended to the launch, "Wickel's not so bad. He's kind of sweet. He's upset about Lipp, that's all."

"I wish he would shut up," replied Doña Teresa, her temper impaired by Mimi's radiance, by Mimi's legs, by the awful fact of Mimi's arrival back on board. "He is not sweet!"

"He's going to order us some cables and a spring. We think the toy needs a spring."

"It needs to be toppled overboard."

"It might be fun. Maybe we don't need a better reason than it's fun."

Doña Teresa peeled off an adhesive glare and taped it to Mimi's forehead. "*Fun!*" She sat down angrily and yanked her long skirt around her legs.

From her mist of elation Mimi recognized the rightness of this outburst. "Please ignore me," she begged.

"I suppose you are famous for your generous nature," said Doña Teresa.

"I'm terrible," smiled Mimi.

And they went away from *Bismarck*'s side, Doña Teresa and the Fregattenkapitän, Mimi and Hans-Adam. *Hood* was after them. The Fregattenkapitän knew it. The news pursued him. He received it absently. His mind lingered on painting, and on a summer's day when he'd argued with his mother on the terrace of a schloss, and drunk warm wine from teacups.

"They are having a show of the Picasso," he explained to Mimi as they motored in to Cleveland. "Picasso," he repeated, this time to Doña Teresa. "The cubistic art."

"I know nothing about it," pronounced Doña Teresa, as if this fact itself ought to give the Fregattenkapitän a second thought. From the depths of his reverie he slid her a pacific glance. "Spanish."

"There is no need to bellow," stated Doña Teresa. The Spanishness of the painter Picasso, she wished the Fregattenkapitän to understand, meant zero to a lady shaped by an English education and several decades in a German battleship.

The launch disgorged them at a marina. They found a taxi, went to the museum.

"I know nothing about it," Doña Teresa advised them again, firmly assigning responsibility for Picasso to the Fregattenkapitän, who wandered ahead of them into the gallery.

Although he shambled, Fregattenkapitän von Prenzlau possessed that old authority that all commanders have: they expect to be obeyed, and this serenity is absolute. The usher didn't even ask him for a ticket. The Fregattenkapitän sailed past him, past the whole long line of Picassophiles. Doña Teresa glided by, perfectly enclosed in her remoteness from the daily run of things in Cleveland. Hans-Adam was unreachably aloof, tapping his fingernail against his teeth and lost in spacious thoughts. Lacquered to his side, Mimi too slid by.

Starved for fifty years, the Fregattenkapitän fell upon the pictures. "Schön," he breathed before them, one after another, sighing and repeating, "schön."

It can't have been easy for the guards, watching as this frail grey figure rummaged in his tunic for cigarettes. They tensed as he patted his pockets for a match. Their faces twitched in dismay as he ripped a twig-sized match along his leg and put it to his cigarette. They plunged to his side. The Fregattenkapitän listened to their remonstrations. He tilted his head and attended them with courtesy. When they'd finished, he took a contemplative drag at his cigarette, exhaled, gestured at a painted oyster, or a fork dashed off by the master's brush. "Schön," he confided to a guard, and to the other, "schön." Then he handed them his cigarette and strolled away.

"The brush," an elderly lady remarked to him as they stood before some pears. "The flatness, but the depth!"

"And what has become of it?" he asked her.

"It has ended."

Doña Teresa fixed this interloper with a predatory eye, and she left. The Fregattenkapitän hauled out a cigarette and began to pat his pockets for a match.

Several miles away a brand new spring, packed in grease, arrived on Bismarck's deck. So did some cables. What could Wickel do? He could do nothing. He loved Lipp. He loved the prince. He must do as they wished. If they wished this toy to work, then work it must. Wickel glared at it. He glared at its dials and its brass, and especially at the hole in the centre, the hole where they would crawl. Wickel's heart was piled to the rafters with every kind of ancient artifact, and loyalty was one of these, and love. But it pained him, this toy, it was too much, and he marched off to snarl at the watch and order them to keep their eyes on the northeast. War! For God's sake, let there be a war!

xviii

RED TABS, BLUE tabs, grey tabs – a mound of tabs rose on Anne's desk. She caught another box, opened it, spilled it onto the pile. Box after box she added to the hill of colored tabs. The wastebasket filled with small grey boxes. She shook the last tab from the final box, and held the empty box close to her face. Flecks of colored cardboard clung to the inside. She smelled it. It didn't matter what color tabs there'd been, every box smelled the same.

The fax line rang. Anne ignored it. A strip of paper curled from the machine to join a tangled heap on the floor. She didn't bother reading the heading: it would be archives. She let it gather in a growing mess. She plunged a fist into the colored mound on her desk and fished out a handful of tabs. She let them dribble back. Next time it was the phone that rang.

"Oh," she exclaimed. She fumbled for it, said hello in a husky voice.

"It's Palango."

"Oh."

"What's wrong?"

"What?"

"Anne. Wake up. You sound half asleep."

"I was just thinking."

"About what?"

"I don't know. Things."

"It's not like you to be vague."

"I know." Anne stirred the pile of tabs with her fist. "It puzzles me too."

"Do you want to know how I'm getting on with the story?"

"I don't actually give a fuck, Mimi."

"Anne!"

"Quiet for a sec." Anne strained to listen. There – she heard it again! Over the phone! The cry of a seabird! She opened her fist; tabs spilled to the floor. "That's a gull!"

"What is?"

"It's just reminded me, that's all." She sprang up and slashed her fist at the pile of tabs, sending a flurry to the floor. "I can *smell* that stupid ship, Mimi." She paced to the window, stretching the phone cord as far as it would go. "Maybe I should get him some cigarettes. I don't know about those cigars."

"Are you all right?"

"Yes," said Anne, "you bet."

"You sound funny."

"I guess it should be cigars."

"They're a little ugly, those cigars."

"Exactly. Otherwise I'm just a row of knuckles with a hairdo."

"Sure, but a hairdo that would launch a thousand ships."

"Bye."

"Anne?" said Mimi. "Anne?"

Port Colborne lies at the south end of the Welland Canal. Anne must have hoped (she had hoped) to intercept the ship as it left the canal. Long before she reached the town she saw *Hood's* foretop, miles distant, the battle cruiser already abroad on Lake Erie. By the time Anne reached Morgans Point *Hood* was well offshore, standing away southwestwards up the lake. A paste of smoke oozed from her stack. Her broken foretop leaned at a sharper angle. The greenhouse seemed about to topple off. Anne heard the muddled thrum of *Hood*'s old engines, the struggling pumps. Viscous water burped from hoses rigged through ports, and surely the battle cruiser listed and went more heavily, inscribing a message legible to Anne's astonished heart, a plain message of love.

"Bit of a lean, what, Guns?"

"Some of her plate came away in that blasted canal," rasped Paget.

Sir Robert shot him a covert glance. "Wrinch will be unhappy. Hard luck. Chap's whole garden canted over at an angle." Paget ignored this. "I believe," Sir Robert ruminated, "I believe he was thinking of the Big Bertha, and perhaps a row of Park's Whopper." The goat was gone. That snake had got it, certainly. Sir Robert faced a future made of green. "Doesn't cheer one, the cucumber, does it, Guns?"

"Keep a sharp eye off the port bow," Paget growled into a bridge telephone. "Watch for smoke."

"Dashed hard," Sir Robert added – a last, sad clutch at the vanished past. "A bit of goat, it's not too much to ask."

"She's got about eight degrees of starboard list on her," Paget frowned. "I shall have to move some pumps."

"Wrinch will be grateful."

"Not if they are his pumps."

A line of six white shapes came suddenly into view, flying across the bow from port to starboard level with the bridge, in perfect order one behind the other, great wings powering them on as they altered course toward a destination far down the shore.

"Swans," gasped Sir Robert. "Trumpeters, what?"

Paget shook his head. "Not large enough. Whistling, more like it." He got his glasses onto them. "Last of the migration, I would think."

"*Cygnus columbianus columbianus*," Sir Robert breathed.

"That's it," said Paget. "Wintered on the Chesapeake, would you say?"

"Oh, very likely." They watched the line of swans as it sank toward the shore. "Marvelous feet," Sir Robert sighed, "marvelously black." They listened to the calling swans. "Smashing, that."

"A sort of whistling bark," said Paget. "The books say it sounds like wow-wow-wow."

"More like a who-who, who-who," mused Sir Robert.

"That's how I'd have put it."

"All the way to the Arctic, that lot." The birds dwindled in the offing, receded, sank. Sir Robert and Paget turned away only when the swans had disappeared, merging with the shore.

"Shy chaps," said Sir Robert. "Very wise of them, I suppose."

Rags of cotton cloud knotted and unknotted on a field of blue. A water breeze blew by, lobbing grenades of freshness into the battle cruiser. A gentle sea ran down from the western end of the lake, two hundred miles away. A wideness of water lay about the ship. Mrs. Wilcox had been heard to hum as they drew away from shore. Crickington swung a driver on the port wing, balancing himself against the tilt. Sir Robert seemed to forget his goat, and even Paget smacked one fist into the other in a hearty gesture, startling Corcoran, the quartermaster.

Anne found a launch to take her out. By the time they reached *Hood*, her confidence had shrunk. Perhaps a straightforward announcement of her love might not be quite the thing. She remembered a time three years before, when she'd removed the glass from a man's hand, told him to pay attention, and presented her convictions. He'd listened, clearly horrified, snatched back his drink and gulped it down. Then he'd muttered something about friendship and escaped.

Paget waited on the bridge.

"You're surprised to see me," said Anne.

"It's not a pleasure I'd looked for." He blinked twice and fiercely rubbed his chin, inspecting his fingers hopefully, as if he would welcome blood. Sir Robert semed to notice nothing. Anne thought he might not know she was there, until he addressed the dog.

"There is to be no surliness with the German lady. I must insist upon it."

Into this knightliness bustled Mrs. Wilcox. "Tea," she announced, and promptly restored the smell of spirits which the breeze had jeopardized.

"I say, Wendy," said Sir Robert, struggling to be brave, "who knows but we might not find a bit of cucumber."

"Mup," ventured Wendy.

"I can't imagine why you've come," said Paget.

"You're angry."

Paget searched for an answer, gave up and tramped out onto the port wing. A narrow, oily creature (a weasel) shot from behind a stanchion and snaked for cover. Paget wrenched a slab of rust from a hatch and flung it hard. It slapped to the deck and flew apart behind the fleeing animal. Two glossy rabbits popped their heads from a clump of gorse and peered at Paget in alarm. Griggs, the yeoman, lowered his binoculars and stared.

"Damn it, Griggs," snapped Paget. "Keep your eyes in your head."

"Aye aye, sir," mumbled Griggs, looking from Paget to Anne to the rabbits.

"Guns," they heard Sir Robert chant, "she's done us the cucumber."

"Stuff the bleeding cucumber," Griggs muttered from behind his binoculars.

"It's that new Green Maiden," Mrs. Wilcox volunteered to the ship at large. "You might tell Sir Robert as Mr. Wrinch prizes them Green Maidens."

"Balls on Wrinch," mumbled Griggs.

"Oh, let it alone, Griggs," Paget snapped.

"Aye aye, sir," Griggs replied, forgetting for the moment who Paget was, and surprised to find him there.

Anne fished out a silver package, bunted it open with her knuckles and offered Paget a thin cigar. He sniffed it, stuck it in his mouth, and raised his eyes to the horizon. "I suppose you think me churlish."

Anne fished out a lighter, lit her own cigar, handed the lighter to Paget. "You just think I'm going to ruin your fun.

Paget concentrated on his cheroot. "The rifling of the guns was ruined long ago. A bush is growing from the cutwater. The flash-proof scuttles are useless. We are awash in any kind of sea." He stared at the back of Griggs's head and took a long pull at his cigar. He looked pleased as he exhaled. "Not an enormous lot of fun."

"If you want to feed me your rigmarole," she replied. "that's fine. It's not going to scare me off."

Paget looked at his cigar. "I don't follow you, I'm afraid."

"Yes, you do." And a grin that had been hiding in her suddenly sprang out, ambushing them both. Paget looked startled, even dismayed, at this surprise attack. Anne let her left eyelid crash down in a shattering wink. "You're just afraid of me, you big doll."

Paget held onto his cigar. "It's a somewhat unusual allegation. I'm not sure I have time to refute it."

"How about a kiss, then?"

"What's this?" came Sir Robert's voice. "Guns, there's relish too."

"Relish up yer arse," growled Griggs.

Paget ground at his chin. "I have already spoken to you, Griggs."

The yeoman jumped. "Aye aye, sir," he barked, amazed.

A bridge telephone rang. Paget let it ring a second time. He forced his eyes to Anne's. "I am not used to any of this," he told her firmly. When the telephone rang a third time he picked it up and listened.

"Foretop, sir," came a tinny voice. "Smoke bearing red one-oh!"

"Can you see anything else?"

"Not yet, sir."

Paget replaced the telephone. He raised his binoculars and swept an arc south past Pennsylvania. Ohio tilted a load of cool bright air onto Lake Erie. Nothing marked that perfect sky. Paget could see no smoke. Visibility from the foretop would be miles greater. In other times he might have sent the crew to stations, but what was the use? *Hood*'s captain crowed about relish while sparrows squabbled at his feet for crumbs. Men searched the ship for a snake. No one would hear the bells, if they rang at all. Paget stepped inside and stopped by the wheel.

"Speed, Corcoran?"

"Six knots, sir, at a guess."

"How's she handling?"

"Not as ginger as I'd like, sir."

Paget dragged out a chart. "Foretop's reported smoke at red one-oh."

Corcoran nodded. "Twenty miles, that'd be, sir, at a guess."

"*Bismarck*," said Paget, stabbing a finger at Cleveland. Nothing else would make that smoke. "She's getting up steam."

"No good falling in the hands," Corcoran sighed. "It'll be a day just to close that range. They'd fall asleep."

"Or wander off," agreed Paget.

"Isn't it the truth, now, sir?"

"I daresay we shall fall apart at the first salvo."

"Oh, aye," Corcoran sounded cheerful. "Sink like a stone."

"Cigar?" said Anne to Mrs. Wilcox. Mrs. Wilcox scrutinized her brown teapot. "If you don't want to smoke it now, you can take it for later."

Mrs. Wilcox pursed her lips, nodded stoutly and slipped a cigar into a pocket of her apron. "You don't have to have tea," she said in a low voice.

Ten minutes later Anne finished an espresso. "You're a genius," she said, replacing the cup on Mrs. Wilcox's tray. "You could measure that in volts."

Mrs. Wilcox moved away from Sir Robert's chair. "Mr. Crickington nicked me one of them machines. He knows as I like a proper bit of coffee."

Anne slipped the package of cigars from her purse and tucked it into Mrs. Wilcox's apron. "I have more."

Mrs. Wilcox fiddled with the tray, then picked it up. "They're a black lot, miss."

"They do seem to have their little oddities."

"They're a black lot," Mrs. Wilcox stepped over Wendy and prepared to leave the bridge. "There's nought as can be done about it."

"There must be something."

Mrs. Wilcox shook her head. "It's historical."

xix

SOME KIND OF warbler had discovered *Bismarck*'s bees. Doña
Teresa rolled her newspaper into a weapon and swiped at a
flash of yellow feathers.

"They are insatiable!"

The birds, grotesquely happy, camped among the vines and
yodeled at the world. On the chipped blue table three blossoms
floated in a bowl. The water trembled as Hans-Adam, on his
knees, wedged a napkin under a table leg. He gave it an experi-
mental push. It wobbled, but not as badly as before.

"The topside lookout has reported smoke in the northeast,"
said Doña Teresa. Hans-Adam sat and helped himself to an enormous slice of cake, hideously brown and studded with chips of
candied fruit. Wickel had found one on sale in Cleveland, and
ordered a gross. Hans-Adam, stuffed so full of Mimi he could
almost float, blew her a cakey kiss. Doña Teresa poured a tar-
thick glob of coffee into a china cup and tried not to grind her
teeth. Hans-Adam stole a glance at Mimi's legs. She re-crossed
them, a task not hindered by the foot-wide strip of wool that was
her skirt. "Smoke in the northeast," insisted Doña Teresa, "probably twenty miles."

"That ship?" said Mimi. "The one that's chasing you?"

Hans-Adam swallowed, wiped his lips. "Chasing – it's not the word I'd use. We're not ready yet, that's all."

"Isn't that a quibble?"

Hans-Adam didn't think so. "We're armed. That implies a willingness to fight." He spoke meticulously, holding a finger upright before his face and wagging it back and forth, like a metronome. "If we're not at the moment fighting, it's because we're waiting for the right time. Classic approach. Von Clausewitz." He arched his eyebrows.

His smugness irritated Mimi, and the way he examined his fingernail. "The thing is," she countered reasonably, "there isn't a war anymore. You're at peace."

"Well as for that, what's peace?"

"Gee, it's been in all the papers," Mimi blinked at him. "You know, people stop driving tanks through each other's cities? Men go home and mow the lawn? People get to keep their arms and legs?"

Hans-Adam smiled at his hands. "Since you're reading the papers so attentively, you'll have noticed that it doesn't matter what countries do. The people never finish with a war."

"Boy," said Mimi, "that's deep. I guess I should be taking notes."

"It's why I thought you were here."

Doña Teresa watched them blissfully, so filled by the helium of their dispute that she almost had to grasp the chair to keep from floating off.

Mimi bit her lip. "We're having a fight, aren't we?"

Hans-Adam shrugged. "I'm just trying to get you to see that if war is an extension of politics, doesn't it make sense that peace might be an extension of war?"

"Is that von Cheeseburger again?"

Hans-Adam tapped his fingernail against his teeth, exactly twice. "I'm not surprised you haven't met these ideas. They don't come up on Larry King."

"Oh, come on!" said Mimi. "This is all part of some fancy *philosophy*? Is that what you're trying to tell me?"

"I wouldn't try to tell you anything."

Mimi closed her eyes and took a deep breath. "All I'm saying is that there's probably some way to settle this."

Hans-Adam tapped his fingernail against his teeth, twice more. "There is of course a way." And at that moment Wickel stamped onto the bridge to report that a boat had attacked them in the night — an attempt to ignite the oil slick around the ship.

"Partisans?" Hans-Adam asked.

Who else? They'd catapulted bottles filled with gasoline into the oil and against the ship itself.

"Casualties?" Hans-Adam asked.

An otter had suffered burns. Lipp was attending it in the sick bay.

"It seems the bakery receipts are now to be enlisted against otters," Hans-Adam rose. "I think they've got the boiler working," he said to Doña Teresa. "I'm going to see what's happening with turret Bruno."

And when he'd left, Doña Teresa said, "Perhaps you do not understand us, my dear."

Mimi leapt up so quickly her chair jumped back and rattled to the deck. "I *love* him!" Her face contorted with distress. "Is it a crime against you that I love him!?"

Doña Teresa touched the starched linen of her blouse. She fumbled for her locket, adjusting it minutely. "You think this is all pointless."

"Of course it's pointless to die! How can death have a point!?"

"Not death!" Doña Teresa put her fingertips to her temples. "Don't say that! I am old! I have no one without the boy!"

Mimi looked at the Fregattenkapitän. "You have *him*," she whispered, seizing Doña Teresa's hand. "You have *him*."

"He cannot belong to me." Doña Teresa's voice was weary. "He belongs to his past."

"Damn it," pleaded Mimi, "that's just a line! It's probably what someone wrote! It doesn't have to be anybody's fate."

"Of course it must be someone's fate. Why else was it written?"

The smoky tomcat slipped from a shadow. Bees drifted about his head. One of them paused to evaluate the cat's huge ears, as if it hoped there might be pollen there. The tom twitched and rubbed his head against some leaves. A shower of petals fell to the deck. The cat made a detour around Doña Teresa and stopped near Mimi, in a patch of sunlight. Doña Teresa gathered her heavy skirt and swished away, her right hand raised, the thumb and middle finger pressed to the corners of her eyes. Mimi would not cry, would *not*, and made herself be still. The tom began to rumble peacefully, and turned his head so Mimi could see how perfectly a pair of yellow eyes could deal with life. Mimi scooped some cake into a saucer and put it on the deck beside the cat. When he was quite ready, he crouched and gave this offering a sniff. A small pink tongue came out and tested it. Then he sat up again and turned his back, and licked his paws as if the whole of Persia waited his command.

Mimi leaned forward and planted her elbows on her knees. "Next time I'll get a tin of tuna."

But when she tried to pat him, he slipped away.

XX

"HEAVIER SMOKE ON that bearing, sir," Corcoran said to Paget. "Foretop thinks she's getting under way."

Sir Robert flew awake. "*Bismarck?*" he gasped.

"It's only smoke," said Paget, angry that Corcoran had spoken out.

"I suppose I may have the bearing?" Sir Robert said.

"Red one-oh."

Sir Robert snatched his binoculars and raised them to a point just off the port bow. "Yes," he murmured, "there you are."

Paget raised his own binoculars. He could see it too, a mark on the horizon, a scratch against the rim of sky. "They will have seen us too, of course."

"We have her," breathed Sir Robert, shifting. A plate with a cucumber sandwich almost slid from his knees.

"Hours yet," said Paget. "Tomorrow daybreak at the earliest." He sounded weary.

Sir Robert moved his glasses slightly downward. "Masses of those chunky little buffleheads right inshore, Guns. *Masses* of them."

Paget swung his glasses down. "Butterballs, some people call them. Tiny chaps."

"*Bucephala albeola*," said Sir Robert. "Nothing like them at home, what? Look how they sit in the water. Almost on top of it."

"Scrappy fellows for their size." Paget sharpened his focus. A flock of smartly patterned black-and-white water fowl bobbed like corks on the water. "Build their nests in trees, bless their hearts."

"Plucky little fellows," Sir Robert agreed. "Dive in a blink, eh?" He sighed and put his glasses in his lap. He noticed the plate and tipped its burden to the deck, where it landed in front of Wendy's nose. The dog examined with evident distaste the bread, the cucumber, a smear of relish. Mastering herself, she lifted her head a quarter of an inch and hoovered it in with a single, muffled "floop."

"We had better close the ship, Guns," Sir Robert gazed at the dog. "Send the men to stations."

"They will only fall asleep."

"Then we shall know where to find them, Wendy."

Anne sat in Paget's cabin, waiting for Mrs. Wilcox's coffee to finish its tantrum in her brain. She decided to calm herself with a cigar. It seemed sensible, just the act of lighting it, as if the physical object and the smoke, together with the act that linked them, constructed some irrefutable logic. Her cell phone went.

"I just refuse to be worried by this," Mimi started right in, "I intend to refuse to be worried by it."

"Have a cigar, Palango. That would be my advice."

"I am going to build my story up carefully. I plan to ignore the war side. It's too obvious. I'm concentrating on the personal side."

"Lucky you."

"The old woman comes from Argentina. She played polo on a women's team. She met Hans-Adam's mother at a polo match in England. They became best friends."

"Where's the mother now?"

"His parents are dead. His father died from being wounded on this ship."

"How?"

"I don't have all the details yet."

"No kidding."

"It's not something we like to talk about."

"Oh, I see. You're both doing the story, are you?"

"Don't be sarcastic with Palango, OK? She's a little fragile."

"Mimi, that broad has a black belt in sex."

"We had a fight."

"That's what the black belt is for. You stun him with sex. Once he's dazed, handcuff him naked to the wall."

"He's pretty serious about this war stuff."

"Gee, imagine that," Anne leaned from the porthole. An otter rolled on its back and crossed its paws. It looked asleep. Anne puffed on her cigar, absurdly content, and squinted at the lake. "I guess you already know we can see your smoke?"

"What do you mean, 'we'?"

"I forgot to tell you. I'm on the *Hood*."

"You forgot to tell me!?"

"That's right."

"You're on the *Hood*!?"

"Stop it, Mimi."

"But I need a base I can re*ly* on! I need your sup*port*! I need you be*hind* me!"

"Tell you what. I'm going to take a drag, and while I'm doing that, you take three deep breaths."

"It's just, I don't know, it's not how we usually work."

"I think we've covered this topic in a general way already. It's a brave new world, my little salami. Nothing is how we usually work."

Mimi wrestled with this bulletin. Anne waited, engrossed in her own contentment. Mimi signaled her capitulation to the new planetary order with a brisk resumption of her tale.

"That toy of his — we tried it out."

"It's working?"

"I don't think so. I crawled in and lay on a canvas sheet and held onto these leather straps."

"That might not have been too bright. All this stuff is pretty old."

"I'm trying to make up with him."

"Try frontal assault."

"They turned it on. It sort of jiggled sideways a bit and stopped. There was smoke."

"Was it fun?"

"Maybe it will be."

"That's a very, very crazy toy. I hope you know what a good angle it is."

"What about you? Are you going to stay there?"

"I don't know. He gave me his room, but he hasn't exactly rolled over so I can scratch his tummy."

"Wear the green pants and that creamy shirt. Soak him with pheromones. Confess that your real name is Desirée."

"You think so?"

"The Palango women have passed this lore down through the generations."

"They are generous to a fault."

"No. They want half of anything you get from CNN."

Fouling the lake with bunker oil the battle cruiser proceeded southwestward. For years her habitat had supported many creatures, like the bright-blue snakes. They'd been a sturdy race, prowling into *Hood* and dining on a kind of snail that lived on hardened oil. Then, two weeks ago, they'd gone. Freshwater had driven them off. It had been hard on the men, watching them cough freshwater from their bodies as they swam back to sea. Their place had quickly filled. A smaller snake discovered the snails, a pale-pink snake banded with narrow bands of iridescent green. The raccoons, desolated by the loss of their bright-blue prey, found this supply of pale-pink bodies. The ecology had settled down.

But now the animals sensed harm. Sir Robert had ordered *Hood* closed for battle. The animals found old routes cut off. Some hint of danger must have accosted them, something that rode downstream in the postal flow of memory from generation to generation. This news went crying through the ark. The pale-pink snakes plunged from companionways. Raccoons pelted upwards, desiring altitude. Some hid out at Wrinch's farm, where the python slept, draped over pipes, digesting goat and dreaming of a pair of aged jaguars that he'd spotted earlier, harmless brothers with coats faded almost white, who'd come aboard as kittens.

Up the lake went *Hood*, a dim Manhattan of a ship. Night came upon her like a load of darkness shoveled down a chute. Anne sat on the bed in Paget's cabin, pulling pages from a file, staring right through them, laying them aside. A ululation rose from the water. Partisans. They'd been there all day, must still be there, coursing beyond the weeds. Another cry rent the night. Anne dug out her phone.

"Red?" she said when Mimi answered. "Desirée again. The natives are restless. It's bugging my ass."

"Desirée," purred Mimi, "dear, sweet Desirée. You were not made for such as this. Your daddy protected you all your life, feeding you nothing but the finest steaks and, for dessert, flans piled high with apricots."

"I detested the apricots," said Anne. "I could never tell Daddy that."

"It would have broken his heart."

"No, he would have put thumbscrews on the chef and strung him in the trees outside my room."

"And now you have called your friend, the beautiful and dangerous Red Palango, because you are unhappy in love, a love for which your daddy could never have prepared you."

"I confess I'm tired of reading this crap. Damn it, I'm here for the sex."

"Where's Paget?"

"Hey, I don't even know where I am."

"They just left you there?"

"He had some things to do."

"Sounds familiar."

"I know he loves me, Red. It can't be just the cigars."

"He must plight his troth."

"He must give up onion sandwiches and take a position in Daddy's firm, selling software." Anne leaned out the porthole. The battle cruiser made an enormous sloshing sound as it labored up the lake.

"He must foresake his terrible, dark love of warfare," Mimi added, "*and* the sandwiches."

"I'm going to find that schmuck."

"Sure. It's your destiny."

Anne felt her way into the dark companionway. Stars twinkled through gaps in the steel. Light seeped inboard from the lake, as if the water had collected light all day and now released it drop by drop back into the air. She thought she heard his voice, and blundered towards it, but lost her way. The smell of plants and earth and animals confused her. She took a step, and fell. Her hands slipped on the greasy deck and she collapsed. It took her hours (it seemed like hours) to find her way back, and when she did get there, what was there anyway, except her filthy clothes, her scraped fists, the private humiliation of her tears?

xxi

THE SUN WAS already high when Hans-Adam fizzed into Mimi's cabin on his toes and bubbled to the porthole. "That smoke, you can see it plainly now!" Mimi turned her head on the pillow and marveled at his profile. A smudge of oil marked his cheek.

She rolled on her side to face him. "Am I beautiful?"

"Sensational!" He kept his eyes on the smoke, eyes alight with excitement that was not excitement about her, and which he carried with him when he left, as he immediately did, yielding his place to the big grey tom, who wafted through the door and paused to take the last remaining shrimp from a saucerful that Mimi'd left for him the night before. He swallowed hard, then stopped to wash his face, and after that, and only then, he uttered a single feline sentence and sprang to the bed, landing at Mimi's feet. With his ears straight forward and his tail straight up he walked up Mimi's leg, waded across her stomach and dumped his body on her chest. There he released a hippopotamus-sized yawn before commencing a steady, thunderous, and hideously shrimp-flavoured purr, right into Mimi's face.

"Oh, yag," she winced. "Men!"

But the tom ignored her.

They'd got the patch on Number Two starboard boiler to hold. They'd got up steam. Lipp felt well enough, stuffed with morphine and pottering about his orchard scrutinizing leaves. He would not hear of bed. Maschinenmaat Nissel decided to re-wire the toy – completely. The Fregattenkapitän, startled by an insight about Rothko (an insight about directness), raised his left hand (hand with signet) above his head and allowed it to descend, small fingertip advanced, so that it touched his head first here, then there. Musikmaat Schreier dispatched a phrase of Schubert across the anchorage. And thus prepared, the battleship *Bismarck* pulled in her anchors and wore her bows around to the west, warped into the channel, put Cleveland firmly at her stern and set out to complete the ascent of Lake Erie.

"I think we should have a talk," said Mimi, arriving at the chipped blue table. She yanked out a chair and sat. Hans-Adam studied an omelette.

"Perfect," he prodded it. "It's perfect." Mimi reached across and tore off half, flinging it away. A posse of hens rounded it up with cries of approval. Hans-Adam shrugged and sank a fork into what remained of the omelette. This time Mimi slid the whole plate away and dumped what remained of the omelette to the foraging hens. She parked the empty plate to one side and banged her forearms on the table. Water slopped from the flower bowl. Doña Teresa adjusted her locket slightly to the right, back left by half, and a final smaller fraction to the right. A bee, insanely brave, ventured out to take a gander at the egg-specked plate. A warbler arrowed in from the vines, and that was that. The Fregattenkapitän restored his signet to the armrest with a "tick." *Bismarck* inched away from Cleveland. The hens galloped off with their booty. Hans-Adam's mood evaporated in an instant. He thrust his chair away and whirled off, with Mimi after him – a pair of electrons

bound by a force that surged between them and that they themselves produced.

Hans-Adam left her behind: *Bismarck* zipped shut behind him.
Mimi listened down a hatch. The ship's last boiler blew like a
calliope. She rushed forward. He was not at turret Bruno, where
Wickel had a dozen hands clearing away the vegetation and starting on the rust. The toy! She stumbled back to the toy. He wasn't
there. She looked inside. On an impulse, she climbed right in.
She could smell the grease from the new spring; the cables they'd
bought to support the sling still had that sheen of newness. She
grasped the canvas hand-straps that hung from above. It was her
first time here alone. A gust of petals shivered past the entrance
hole. A pair of nesting birds (warblers?) made inquiring noises
from somewhere high in the machinery. Mimi started to cry.
Angrily, she kicked at a switch beside the opening. The toy gave
a great cough: the canvas sling sank about a foot, then launched
her straight up. A horn honked loudly. A shower of straw fell
in Mimi's face, and the birds (definitely warblers) shrieked and
tore about among the steel braces. Mimi fell back into the sling,
bouncing hard off one of the poles that supported it along each
side. The toy subsided with a gasp of smoke. Mimi let go the
straps and banged her fists against the poles. A red face appeared
in the opening.

"You have the pain!?" Wickel bellowed.

"No," sniffed Mimi, snaking out. Wickel glared at the toy.
Mimi smoothed her skirt. "It's OK, really," she sniffed, "thanks."

She tracked him down at the orchard. He was standing intent
as a heron, his eyes locked on the bench where Lipp sat stunned
by apple blossom, blossoms in his hair, blossoms on his hands.
Mimi tried to take Hans-Adam by the fingers; he shoved his hands
into his tunic pockets. More petals shivered down to join the little
heaps that decorated Lipp's shoulders. A bright green caterpillar

clambered through this fragrant litter, utterly dazed, its gummy feet dislodging nervous avalanches colored pink.

"He's dying," Hans-Adam said, "I think."

"Has he seen a doctor?"

Hans-Adam shook his head. "And now he won't."

"Do you know what it is?"

"We think cancer, but maybe not."

Mimi searched Hans-Adam's face. "I'm glad at least we're talking."

"Glad?" A petal landed on his nose, and he slapped it away. "It's another disease, this talking. You are addicted to it."

"It's a disease for people to communicate?"

"Communicate! That's what I mean! You make it sound like something moral, like confession."

Mimi picked a shard of pink from his lapel. "I don't know about moral."

He brushed her hand away. "Don't be arch, Mimi. In the circumstances, it's revolting." He strode to the bench and sat and brushed petals from Lipp's hair. Mimi took the other side of Lipp, and when Hans-Adam picked up one of the old man's hands, Mimi picked up the other. A petal drifted down and lodged behind Lipp's ear. Mimi plucked it out.

"I don't know how you can say you love me."

"At this moment I don't."

"And what am I supposed to do!? Take up knitting!? Sit here with my mouth shut while you put on the helmet with the horns and stand in the bow with your spear!?"

"You get nothing right," he said coldly. "We're too much for you." He put his hand against Lipp's cheek, then sprang to his feet and left the orchard. Mimi watched him go. He disappeared into a hatch near the after fire-control station. She took a handful of petals from Lipp's shoulder and pressed them to her face.

"This relationship," she said, "it's in real trouble."

Lipp moved his jaw. It made a slippery, wooden sound that might have signified assent.

Evening quickened into night among the apple trees. The lights of Cleveland stood upon the water and the land, two masses of lights. Flights of bats emerged from crevices to seize in their teeth the dragonflies that combed the orchard for mosquitoes. *Bismarck* proceeded into the west, following the outward flow of day as it dragged creation with it, into the purple duchy of the night. And on the starboard quarter, too distant to be seen and anyway now lost in that ravishing domain of dark, gathering dreams of war about her as she came, the battle cruiser *Hood*.

xxii

CRICKINGTON SHOULDERED HIS clubs and stamped aft to the fourth tee. Tricky business, this golfing at night. Couldn't shoot a chap for trying.

A clump of birches grew behind the forward stack. Cricking-ton pushed his tee into a patch of grass and studied the trees. If you got off a nice hook with a four-iron, you could dodge that copse and make it to the green in one shot. If you couldn't, then your ball went into the rough, a wilderness of mouldered iron. Cricking-ton swung. He heard the ball clatter somewhere. Damn it, could-n't see a thing. He shouldered his bag. Might as well go home and face the woman. She'd been at him all day about his hair.

"I think that wants a bit of trimming, Mr. Crickington," she said as soon as he came in. He dumped his clubs resignedly. Mrs. Wilcox rummaged in her apron, found the big tortoise-shell comb. Crickington took his place in the chair. She dragged the comb through his thin hair.

"I'm afraid we shall be at it by dawn, Mrs. Wilcox."

She draped a sheet around his shoulders. "I'll just tidy up around the ears."

"It'll ruin the greens," he sighed. "Ruin them."

She got the scissors going. "We'll have you looking smart, Mr. Crickington. That's something, eh?"

"It is."

"You officers has got to set an example." She gnashed the scissors back and forth in front of a rebellious hair, and cut it. "Can't have the ship's officers looking dowdy. It wouldn't do."

"It wouldn't do at all, Mrs. Wilcox."

"Them Jerries," she squinted at Crickington's head, "them Jerries has a reputation for smartness."

"It's true."

"Well, then. What's this, eh? Isn't this the Royal Navy?"

"It is exactly that."

Thus vindicated, Mrs. Wilcox lined up another hair and felled it with a single snip.

"You do a pretty good job of avoiding me," said Anne. Paget sat on one of the faded sofas – man and furniture a perfect match. Anne sat beside him and tapped his knee with a five-pack of cigars. "You look as if somebody's wrung you out like a rag." A lamp with a silk shade cast an improbably elegant light onto the carpet, warming the reds. Paget accepted a cigar. They performed their ritual of lighting, and retreated into smoke.

Finally Paget said, "I've told the bosun to arrange a boat for morning."

Anne sketched a gesture with the cigar. "You're going somewhere?"

"It's no good your staying on." He raised his eyes from the floor to her lap. "Surely you see that?"

"I'll tell you what I see," Anne said through a tangle of smoke. Her pale skin reddened. "I see you haven't grasped that I always decide for myself where I go and when." She made a sweep with her cigar. "You can tell the bosun not to bother with a wake-up call, unless he's bringing me breakfast in bed."

"Of course you'd be angry." He sounded sad.

"Oh, for *Christ's* sake, Paget. Why don't you just kiss me?"

Paget picked a shred of tobacco from his tongue. He examined it, then put it back in his mouth and chewed it. Anne shook her head. "I hate it when you do that."

Paget surveyed the lamplight on the carpet. "Men who live without women: we do become repugnant."

"That's just your way of turning all this into a boy's club. You make fun of the secret handshake, but damned if you'll show it to me. Maybe I'll get the message I'm intruding, and leave."

"We shall catch them soon, you know," Paget said tiredly. "That's all. We shall catch them. When we do, there will be a fight. Silly for you to be aboard."

"And that's what's silly about it, that I'm on board?"

Paget exhaled a cloud of smoke and watched it seethe in the incandescence. He got up and went to a porthole. A formation of white shapes took up position in the night air, keeping perfect station on the ship. "Ring-billed," said Paget, "or possibly Herring Gulls."

Anne stayed where she was. "I'm not going. If that ruins your fun, too bad."

"You've said that before," he turned back into the cabin, "about its being fun. You have a strange idea of a battle."

"No, I'm sorry. I didn't mean it that way."

Paget made a gesture with his cigar, a smoky shorthand scribble of pardon.

"Oh, don't be so *generous*," Anne steamed. "This *place*! It's as if I have to wade around knee-deep in contrition!" She bit hard on her cigar, and went right through. Her eyes widened in surprise. She pondered the pieces, one with a hot ash, the other damp. Paget removed another scrap of tobacco from his mouth. This time he discarded it, flicking it through the porthole. A gull peeled away and dropped to investigate.

"They are fighting all around us, you know. On the water and ashore."

"You give them an excuse," responded Anne, squashing the pieces of cigar into a brass ashtray.

Paget witnessed this, appalled. "Here, just trim that end, why don't you? There's plenty left." Anne made a disgusted noise. Paget tore his pained expression from the mashed cigar. "You say we give them an excuse to fight. No one needs an excuse to fight."

"And that's OK, then? It's a guy thing?"

"I'm not certain that's what I've said."

"Well, please, let's try to be certain! Don't let's stop our war on a quibble!"

"Men hate each other," Paget stated. "If you want it plainly, that's how it is. Men have a need for enemies, so they hate each other."

"'They'?"

Paget reached outside and stubbed his cigar delicately against the hull. When he'd finished, he touched the butt to make sure it was out, and put it carefully in his pocket. "For my part, I would have to insist it's nothing personal."

"You don't have to insist on anything at all," said Anne. She sat with her knuckles arranged in her lap, amazingly demure. "Go ahead and kill them, my sweet. It's what we're here for. As long as you're home in time for dinner, that's all we girls care about."

Paget stopped at the door and frowned. "I rarely know what to say to you."

"Just say, 'Bye, honey.'"

Night, glorious night. Old men rummaging in cupboards for biscuit tins. Lake Erie heaving past, draining a vast watershed through its basin at a million gallons a second. Storms come bowling out of the Ohio Valley. Tonight a tag of weather frisked about, sucking in its cheeks and blowing out. It did not vex the warships. Darkened for battle they stood on through the troubled lake, a pair of wayward cities sloshing on to war.

xxiii

A T DAYBREAK THE warships came upon each other. Neither noticed this at first. Musikmaat Schreier, posted in *Bismarck*'s foretop with the strictest instructions from Wickel, had spent his watch examining a purple 10-kroner Austrian stamp of 1922, portrait of Schubert, which Maschinenmaat Nissel had traded for a case of schnapps. Musikmaat Schreier had coveted this stamp for fifty years. As for Nissel, he slumped at his post, humming snatches of nursery rhymes that blew unchecked through cracks in his brain. Nissel hummed and drank, and Number Two starboard boiler went to hell.

Stabsobermaschinist Merz ought to have detected this, for *Bismarck* was no longer under way. She was stopped dead. But the Stabsobermaschinist was perched in a corner of the engine room, lost in the score of Schubert's Trout Quintet. He was a cellist of unsurpassed oafishness, was Merz, but he had a hopeful heart.

"Nissel!" Schreier barked down the voice-pipe when the sound of Merz's scraping drifted up. "See to your engines. They are ill."

"It is I, Herr Musikmaat," came Merz's sorrowful reply. "I beg your pardon, Herr Musikmaat."

"Fah!"

Musikmaat Schreier stuffed a rag in the voice-pipe, arranged his shining boots before him, and concentrated on the beauty of the purple Schubert 10-kroner. Nissel had also alluded to a 25-kroner green, portrait of Bruckner, from the same series. Schreier was not so fond of Bruckner. It might look nice with the Schubert, though. All in good time.

Hans-Adam had spent the whole night on the bridge in a tortured shuttle from instrument to instrument, his face bathed in green luminescence, recognizing nothing. Doña Teresa had fled from this agony, unable to witness it. Wickel would have liked to take Hans-Adam in his arms and kiss him. He supposed he couldn't. The Prince zu Westerwald stared at the dawn. He took another pace and stopped by Wickel. "The girl," he said at last, and shrugged.

Wickel blew out his cheeks and expelled a sympathetic breath. Moreover he rolled his eyes, an extravagance for Wickel.

"They understand nothing about war."

Alas, this was true, Wickel's face proclaimed.

"It's a lost cause, trying to talk. You get nowhere."

Wickel thrust out his lower lip. The lip agreed. Useless to even try, it said.

"I just don't know."

Of course not.

"They are like mules."

One of life's verities.

"Is a man to give up war?"

Appalling!

"She'll feel more reasonable after breakfast."

One may be certain of it.

The Fregattenkapitän too noticed the prince's confusion, but decided to ignore it. What could one do? Precisely nothing. Also there was the pressing fact that *Bismarck* was adrift. Not even the murderous accretions of age and tinned peaches could prevent the Fregattenkapitän from knowing this. The cadences of his ship's decline had settled in his bones, and were as much a part of him as the memory of a battered schloss where his mother and the Margrafin had paused to admire something Dutch and clever in the gallery, while the Margrave had clapped the young von Prenzlau on the back and taken him to see the sabre that the Margrave's grandfather had swung at Austerlitz. In this way war and art moved side by side through the airy ruminations of the Fregattenkapitän. His life had been pressed by the fingertips of both, and marked by their prints, so that the whorls of one might be the whorls of the other. Hans-Adam had not this reverie to sustain him, but only his youth, when he stepped onto the starboard wing and stared across six narrow miles at the enormous approach of *Hood*.

The battle cruiser loomed right there on the starboard beam, impossibly close, a mountainous wraith of devastation and decay. Hans-Adam stumbled back. He gasped for breath. Nothing had prepared him for this sight. Here came his enemy in a slick of oil and weeds, guns awry, flakes of rust drifting into the sludge that trailed at her waterline, her bridge lost in climbing plants – a fortress whose battlements toppled into the encroaching forest. Hans-Adam's eyes began to mist. He thrust his hands behind his back, tilted his chin at *Hood*, and rose up on his toes. "Well," he forced himself to say, and pressed his lips together to prevent a sob. He rocked away, found the alarm button, pounded his fist down hard. A horn began its hectic wail.

"What on earth?" murmured Sir Robert. The alarm dragged him out of sleep. Downwind of *Bismarck*, at that range, the enemy's tocsin came as loudly as if it had come from *Hood* herself. "Guns?"

"I don't like the sound of that, Mr. Crickington," said Mrs. Wilcox, "I don't like the sound of that at all."

Crickington sighed. "Trouble, I shouldn't wonder."

"They'll be wanting you on the bridge." She dragged out her comb and ran it through his hair.

"This place drives me crazy," Mimi said into her phone. "Do you hear that noise?"

Anne struggled through a fog of interrupted sleep. "They want to kill each other, Mimi," she mumbled. She noticed a tray beside her bed, and touched a finger to the coffee pot. Still hot. "Maybe there's a rule that they have to ring a buzzer first," she filled a cup. She would have to order a whole case of cigars for Mrs. Wilcox. The woman was a miracle.

"Now he won't even speak to me," said Mimi.

Anne lifted a piece of toast from a silver rack. Stone cold. You couldn't get everything right. She sipped the coffee. "Do they give you breakfast over there?"

Mimi ignored her. She interrupted her pacing long enough to pluck a dead bloom from the window box. "It's violence, when men treat you like that," she insisted. "It's abuse. There's a word for it, and that's the word."

"No, that's not the word," said Anne. "There are right words for things, and the word for that thing would be 'tiff'. Abuse is a different class of beast."

"Male domination. Same thing."

"*Not* the same thing." Coffee slopped onto Anne's knuckles as she shoved the cup lopsidedly onto the saucer. She sat up. "Damn it, Mimi." She swung out her legs and planted her feet on the floor. "I wish you would be *tidier* with what you say." She propped the phone between her head against shoulder, and yanked her nightgown over her knees. "You're having a fight with your boyfriend. Just stop *announcing* it, will you? It's not the main event out here."

"Maybe it is. Maybe our problems with these guys are a metaphor for the bigger thing."

"That's pretty pat, Mimi, even for you."

"Oh sure, insult me. I'm trying to understand them, and you insult me for it."

"I already understand them. They're a pair of black-hearted bastards who intend to kill each other. Full stop."

Mimi stared at a mass of dangling roots. She'd pulled so hard at a bloom that a whole begonia had come loose. She tried to stuff it back. "It's true. They're sort of old-fashioned, aren't they."

"I wish it were that simple." Anne peered inside the coffee pot. A thick sediment remained. She upended the pot. The residue dribbled into her cup. "Listen, Palango, what's the point? Who cares what we think? It's not as if we have a discourse going here. If he's bugging you, pound him one, that's my advice."

"I don't know, Desirée. It's not how we were taught to build relationships."

"Get with it, Palango. My daddy always said, if they give you trouble, grab them by the scrotum."

"I just think he loves me, and if he does, he'll listen to reason."

Anne contemplated the tray, with its linen cloth splotched with coffee, a small calamity on the snowy surface of civility. "Is that what this is about, we're supposed to be improving them? Making them see something?"

"I guess we disagree about this," said Mimi hopelessly.

"Everything that's happened so far in the world disagrees with you, Mimi."

"I hate thinking that."

"I'm hanging up. That horn is driving me nuts."

"Maybe it's a fire drill."

"Oh, right. Or recess."

Anne hung up.

"Meow?" asked the grey tom from the door, flooding the cabin with the pure, perplexed, and overwhelming query of his big round yellow eyes. "Meow?"

But Mimi didn't know.

Alarms rang in both ships now, bells and hooters and horns. They might mean anything. Off Bermuda once a squall had sprung from a clear sky and run amok in a patch of melons on the foredeck. So wild had been Wrinch's grief that Griggs, standing watch on the port wing, had rung the main battle alarm and sent the ship to stations. Another time it was Crickington, enraged by a nasty slice from the fourth tee. *Bismarck* too. Doña Teresa, in a moment of fury over some cloddishness of Wickel's, had made a sighting report to the Fregattenkapitän, who did not believe her, but ordered a siren anyway and sent a gun crew into turret Bruno: anything for peace. And so, like boys who've all cried 'wolf!' too many times to be believed, the sirens wailed fruitlessly.

Billings, Warrenhook, and Gaspard-Smythe should have been framing *Bismarck* in their sights, aiming *Hood*'s main battery at the enemy. Instead they were locked in wrathful litigation.

"I cannot believe it, Warrenhook," fumed Billings, "that a chap I went to school with would stoop to this." He clutched a frantic turtle and shook it under Warrenhook's nose. "You substituted Edna in the sixth." Warrenhook smiled at his grimy boots and did not dispute it. "Edna," raged Billings, "is a three-year-old."

"Five," murmured Warrenhook.

"Three!" roared Billings, and he turned to Gaspard-Smythe. "Steward, I lodge a protest!"

"I say," said Gaspard-Smythe, attending the distant sound of bells, "that's not action stations, is it?"

"What the bloody hell do I care!?" shouted Billings, thrusting the desperate Edna into one of the swampy turtle pens.

xxiv

MIMI APPEARED ON *Bismarck*'s bridge determined to open a dialogue. That's how she put it: "We need to open a dialogue." Hans-Adam looked alarmed. "Let's start at the beginning," Mimi proposed, "and talk this out."

Hans-Adam made himself into a statue of Prussian formality and gazed at her lips. "Please accept my apology. My behavior was inexcusable."

Mimi bit her cheek. His exhilaration was plain to see. It cheated her. "You agree?"

Hans-Adam ajusted his eyebrows. "There's a chance I'll be distracted," he tilted his head at *Hood*.

Mimi frowned at the battle cruiser. "Is that what all those bells are for? It looks like it might sink. They're not going to shoot, are they?"

"I think they will," he clasped his hands behind his back and straightened his arms. "If they can."

"Can they?"

"Of course." He moved his shoulders, making his tunic neater. "Maybe."

Mimi looked at his chin. "You need a shave." Not many paths of conversation led away from that remark, as Mimi recognized, so she added, "And in case you've forgotten, I love you."

Hans-Adam tightened his grip behind his back. He rose on his toes and studied the maintop stays, which had begun to vibrate in the freshening breeze. "Thanks."

"Oh, you!" She took his face in her hands and kissed him on the lips. "You don't even know what to do with your tongue!"

And she stalked away.

"Enemy in sight," boomed Griggs.

"Steady as she goes," Sir Robert said to Corcoran. For once the air around Sir Robert smelled of air.

"Steady as she goes, aye aye, sir."

"Weave if she fires."

"Weave if she fires, aye aye, sir."

Anne said to Paget, "I wouldn't have thought there'd be much weaving."

"We are somewhat past it," he agreed.

Gorgeous insects with bodies like shards of glass, dragonflies and darters, appeared and disappeared among the plants. Alongside, a pair of otters erupted into a family of snakes. A Caspian tern banked sharply, plunged, and flapped away with a banded snake writhing in its beak. A few miles away slumped *Bismarck*.

"I find it hard to believe you actually plan to attack that ship," said Anne.

"Still, it is our purpose."

"A nutty purpose."

"At any rate, a clear one."

Anne stepped right against him and gripped him fiercely by the sleeve. "I find you infuriating, Paget. I don't think you're indifferent to me."

"Try a round, then, Guns, shall we?" called Sir Robert.

In both ships shreds of data poked about in disarray. A report on wind speed and wind direction made its way along a speaking tube that ended where a shell had sliced it. Ship's speed, enemy's speed, ship's course, enemy's course, range, closing speed, air temperature: some of these were recorded, some not. Some of the men went smartly to their stations, grinning savagely. Others forgot the whole thing instantly and went back to cooking snails. Stokes-Lipton, sub-lieutenant and gunner, made his way in a pleasant haze to the forward fire-control position, and pulled on his headphones.

"Enemy in sight bearing Red one-oh," he heard. "Report when closed up. All quarters with CPBC and full charges load!"

"Hullo?" Stokes-Lipton responded softly.

"Oh, *come* along, Stokes-Lipton. Use proper procedure, can't you?"

"Yes," said Stokes-Lipton affably. Then he removed his headphones and stumbled outside to look for his slave, Ferryman. The order to load with Common Pointed Ballistic Capped, an armor-piercing shell with a pointed nose, must go unexecuted. Stokes-Lipton wanted Ferryman.

"Stokes-Lipton?" crackled the headphones as they swung from a knob. "Are you there, Stokes-Lipton?" A pause. "I can't hear him," the headphones crackled again. "Bloody wiring's rotted out." The headphones crackled once more, and went silent.

In *Bismarck* the gunner Henck peered through his gunsight in the after fire-control position. Efficiently he centred his yellow *wandermark* on the base of *Hood*'s superstructure. Not that either of *Bismarck*'s after batteries would fire. They would not. Nor would they train or elevate. This didn't matter. Henck centred the *wandermark* because it was his job. He did it with a quick, practised twiddling, exactly the same precision that he used to light his cherished meerschaum pipe or milk his little Jersey cow, Heidi, tethered by day in a patch of sweetgrass aft of turret Caesar and, by night, bedded down in amazing luxury in the turret Dora gunhouse beside the attentive Henck.

XXV

A T MID-MORNING A flock of scaup – thousands of them – rose from shallow water inshore and flew out to the ships. From the distant woods came a mass of owls to join them, horn-headed, swift, hooting as they came, birds with a forest intentness in the way they flew. Doña Teresa ignored this avian lunacy. They were birds – what of it? She corrected the position of her locket. It had strayed a zillionth of a millimetre. She pointed a belligerent glance along the bridge at Hans-Adam and Mimi.

"It is ridiculous," she informed the Fregattenkapitän in a low voice, "that this person should believe the prince to be interested in someone of her type."

"She is of the female type," the Fregattenkapitän noted softly. "This is the principal requirement of the male type."

"She is no one!"

"She is a woman, Madame."

"The Prince zu Westerwald's house is a great house!" proclaimed Doña Teresa. "It is," she gestured helplessly, "a princely house." She put down a Meissen cup with such force that the handle came off. She looked at it in horror. "The last of your mother's cups," she gasped.

"Please, it is nothing," the Fregattenkapitän lifted his ring and let it drop. "An object, nothing more."

Wickel exploded onto the bridge and began to shout a catalogue of *Bismarck*'s failings, including an inability to steer as a result of lying dead in the water. Also her guns could not be trained, there being no hydraulics to speak of. Wickel pointed out that all this had some urgency, what with an enemy closing on the starboard beam, and he must further advise the Fregattenkapitän that it was by no means certain that Matrosenhauptgefreiter Lipp could withstand an enemy broadside. The Fregattenkapitän received this report calmly, remembering to inquire after Lipp. Wickel informed his commanding officer that there was no reasoning with the Matrosenhauptgefreiter, who would not budge from the orchard, and that therefore he, Wickel, requested permission to supply Lipp with the last of the morphine. The Fregattenkapitän acceded, and noticing Doña Teresa's acute distress, made a request of his own.

"Something may be done about this cup?"

Wickel plucked the pieces from Doña Teresa and examined them fiercely. He looked from the fractured cup to the crumpled face of his adversary. Doña Teresa straightened her shoulders and looked away. She would not plead, not even for this last relic of the Fregattenkapitän's sunlit childhood. Wickel recognized her defiance, how she held herself away from him. He made a noise like "bah" (it was "bah"), pocketed the Meissen and stamped from the bridge.

"What do you make of those owls, Guns? *Bubo virgianus?*"

"Oh, without a doubt."

Sir Robert's binoculars swept the enemy battleship. "Look at those wings!"

"Four-foot span, I should think."

"Wonderful killers, utterly silent."

"First primary feather on each wing is serrated. Baffles the air-flow. Eliminates the vortex noise, or so one is told."

"They cannot be after those scaup, eh?"

"Wouldn't be their diet."

"What's it all about, then?"

Paget lowered his glasses. "I'm afraid it's not something we'll be able to look into."

Sir Robert blushed. "No, of course not. War, what? Best get on with it."

Wrinch appeared. "Them radishes is as good as gone, sir," he informed Sir Robert. His face hung sadly around his pipe. "No pumps, no water. No water, no radishes. It's nature's way, sir, and there's no two ways about it."

"My dear fellow," murmured Sir Robert, shaken by this grim account. He glanced nervously in Paget's direction before replying. "After all, we are at war. I suppose you will not deny it?"

"I don't know about that, sir," Wrinch was steadfast. "All I know is, them radishes is as good as gone. No pumps, no water. No water, no radishes. Plain as the nose on your face, sir."

"Can't you get a bucket or something?" Sir Robert pleaded.

"No bucket," was Wrinch's flat reply. Something iron ran through Wrinch, and that something had welded itself to pumps.

"Enemy in sight!" bawled Griggs, surfacing into the Lake Erie morning. "Battleship adrift, fine on the starboard bow!"

"Thank you, Griggs," said Paget.

"What!?" shouted Griggs, not recognizing Paget, startled to find him there.

"Be quiet, Griggs."

"Them cukes'll go too," Wrinch shook his head, married to the whole truth.

"Damn it, man," Sir Robert burst out, "why have we not been able to keep a chicken in this ship!? Are we to be spared *nothing*!? Can you tell me that!?"

"No pumps, no cukes," recited Wrinch. Here was truth enough, and Wrinch would not be led from it. Sir Robert crumbled. Even the dog Wendy adopted a haunted look. "Crickington," Sir Robert gargled helplessly, "get a pump to Wrinch, then, can't you?"

xxvi

MUSIKMAAT SCHREIER LIFTED his gaze from the Schubert 10-kroner, glanced from the foretop and recognized *Hood*. At that very moment the first of the British battle ensigns broke from the foretop yard. Schreier sucked in his breath, admiring how the great ensign stood out whitely, even festively, above the disheveled ship. Profoundly moved, he put away the purple stamp, took up his violin, and began to serenade *Hood*. It was something gay and sprightly, of his own invention, and delivered to the breezes quite *vivace*. The violin itself shone with a ruby light as the sun of that spring morning struck its deep Cremona varnish. Schreier's notes flew out upon the air, and also made their way, through a hole in the rusted voice-pipe, all the way to Merz. Seizing his cello, Merz attempted to accompany the Musikmaat, and to hell with Number Two boiler.

xxvii

M IMI CALLED ANNE. "Can you talk?" she asked when
Anne answered. "I couldn't stand it there a second longer!
I'm back in my room. I couldn't stand it up there. Can you talk?"

"Oh, settle down."

"Did you know they're going to try to fire these things!?"

Anne sighed. "It's rather beautiful, this cabin. It's surprising,
isn't it?"

"What is? You're not making sense, Anne."

"I'm not trying to make sense. There's no sense to be made.
That's where we go wrong, trying to make sense of what's going
on. To hell with it, Mimi. Might as well bang our heads against the
wall. So I'm just telling you this cabin is beautiful, and leave it at
that. My big observation for the day is that they've filled a vase
with wildflowers and put it on the desk. Sunlight is pouring in."

"They're treating us like dirt, Anne."

"No, they're not. They didn't invite us along for the ride."

"They don't have to invite us. That's not how it works.
Haven't you read the manual? If you love somebody, you're
allowed to just show up."

"Well, that's what we did, and here we are. I guess the manual
doesn't say anything about a guarantee."

"And that's your contribution to this debate?"

"I don't have a contribution to this debate. I'm not even in the debate. I gave the debating team back their T-shirt. I'm going to have a bath instead."

The grey tom paraded into Mimi's cabin, twitched his tail once, and strolled across to Mimi. "Mrow?" he wondered. "Greow?" Mimi reached down her hand and let him sand it with his tongue.

"So you're just giving up?"

"You bet," said Anne.

"Have you got a private tub?"

"Uh-huh. And I brought some of those new glucose pellets with me. You drop them in the water. Your skin is like silk after."

Mimi walked into the little bathroom. The tom padded in behind. "I've decided to change my eyes," she cradled the phone against her ear as she studied her face in the mirror. "I'm going totally new on the eyes. If he wants war, he'll get war."

"Mrrip?" said the tom.

"Go easy on the eyes," Anne warned. She noticed a fresh sheet clipped to Paget's easel. Another seascape, like the others except for a shoulder and arm, viewed from behind and placed in the left foreground, barely edging into the picture. A woman?

"It's a new kind of purple," Mimi examined the mascara box. "Evening Leopard. I'd forgotten I had it."

Anne studied the watercolor. Definitely, a woman. "He probably likes you the way you are."

"Physically, sure. I think it's all he likes — my body." The tom leaned against her legs.

"Prrrow," he said distinctly. "Frrrow."

A fragment of Schreier's playing drifted into Mimi's phone. Anne heard it. "What's that music?"

"I don't know," said Mimi. Schreier's notes pranced by on the breeze. "Maybe somebody's playing a tape."

"Sounds like a violin."

"I told him I loved him," said Mimi, "even though he treats me like scum."

"I think I'll draw that bath."

"Call you back," said Mimi as Hans-Adam stuck his face around the door. The tom evaporated. Hans-Adam raised his chin, unable to suppress his excitement. His hands were locked behind him. He displayed an elaborate interest in the light switch, unclasping his hands long enough to flick it. The light went on. He shot a look of triumph at Mimi, who sank onto the bed. Hans-Adam paused at the window box and poked a finger at the limp begonia.

"You've got to water these."

"You do the gardening column here?"

Hans-Adam rose to his toes and tapped a fingernail against his teeth. His mood intoxicated him. So did the smell of soap and cotton clothes that came from Mimi. "It's war at last!" he exhaled.

"I thought you were already at war. I thought this was a war*ship*."

This was too much, this tone that Mimi took. Hans-Adam had been born a prince; in rank he was an officer; in love, alas, a schoolboy. He snatched the mascara box from Mimi's fingers, snapped it open, and boldly applied a stripe of Evening Leopard to Mimi's cheek.

"Ah!" cried Mimi.

A flush rose up Hans-Adam's neck. He nodded formally. "Yes," he said, examining his fingers.

"Oh," Mimi gasped. They faced each other, a pair of torches ready for the match.

"Well," Hans-Adam lifted his shoulders, relieved by the enormity of his act.

"Here," said Mimi, "let me help you." She took the mascara and quickly applied a series of strokes to the tip of Hans-Adam's nose.

"I understand," he declared with a little bow. With scrupulous courtesy he borrowed her brush. He placed a patch of purple beneath her left ear. He smoothed it onto her neck. The softness of her skin amazed him. He marveled at the pulse of blood in her neck, at the impossible delicacy of her throat, at the rise of her breasts inside the loosely buttoned shirt. He didn't even notice the shudder that ran through *Bismarck* as her engineers struggled with Number Two starboard boiler. He was lost in his study of that miraculous fabric, Mimi's skin. She put two fingers to her neck and touched them lightly to the smudge of mascara. Hans-Adam presented her with a courtly, downcast smile. When he spoke his tone was chivalrous.

"It becomes you very well."

"Thanks," said Mimi. He had fabulous eyelashes. She wanted to kiss him — just kiss him hard. She extracted her brush from his fingers and drew a small square on his chin. She stood back and squinted at it. "Perfect," she confessed, "it's perfect."

High above them in the foretop, Musikmaat Schreier finished playing his own composition and fell with such immaculate sympathy upon a passage of Schubert that Doña Teresa forgot her guilt about the Meissen and remembered dawn on the pampa. Stabsobermaschinist Merz bellowed at a stoker to be silent. He thrust his ear to the voice-pipe. He listened. A revelation struck him, an apocalypse: never could he accompany such faultless bow-work. He put away his cello and shuffled off to seize a spanner and join his mates. Schubert had his servant; *Bismarck* needed hers. Soon another belch of tar-thick smoke crawled through the ship.

Hans-Adam noticed only Mimi's lips, a vein that throbbed in her neck, a drop of perspiration glinting in the indentation of her collar-bone. His arms enfolded her. Their faces came together in a purple smear. Around them slumped the broken ship, her lungs wasted by years, teeth adrift in her mouth, her rotted pectorals stirring in the current of Lake Erie as she labored to get under way. *Hood* came on through those waters, trailing a forest of water-weed that terrified the fish. She neared her enemy, and now her superstructure rose beyond the window box, beyond that grip of purple-fingerprinted limbs that stiffened now as arm by arm and leg by leg the lovers' bodies waxenly collapsed, drops from a melted candle, into a twisted contour of exhausted love.

xxviii

PAGET STEPPED INTO the cabin. "I should warn you, we shall be going into action."

Anne finished wrapping her wet hair in a turban of towel and sat with her fists in her lap. "Oh, come on. You just heard I was taking a bath. Either that or you're looking for a cigar."

He noticed the vase of wildflowers. "Those are rather pretty, aren't they?"

"They're glorious."

"Have you got one, by the way?"

"One what?"

"A cigar."

"They're in my bag over there. Just fish one out."

"Well . . ."

"Oh, go ahead." And it did make her preposterously happy, watching him paw through her purse. "If you and I survive when this tub sinks, I'm going to buy a bungalow in the country for you and me."

Paget got the cigar going. "A bungalow would suit me, would it, Smythe?"

"You have no idea."

He pointed the cigar vaguely at a boat of partisans coursing past the ship. "But surely . . ."

"Your war, you mean? That's just the next cut on the bungalow

CD. What's the point of fighting if there's no picket fence to paint when you get home?"

He examined the cigar. "I've missed these."

Anne buried her hands in the towel and rubbed her hair furiously. "Why don't you send the Germans a message? They probably like a smoke as much as you."

"I think we couldn't, as we mean to kill each other."

"I wish you wouldn't shrug," she pulled the towel from her head and used it to conceal her hands. She unnerved Paget: her wet hair, the freshness of her skin after a bath, her bare feet on the carpet. Her breasts rose and fell inside the cotton bathrobe. Paget focused on the budding ash of his cigar.

"I must get back on deck."

"You put me in your picture, didn't you?"

Paget glanced at the easel. "One shouldn't make too much of that. It's just a hobby, I'm afraid."

"You're afraid of a lot. Hell, you're afraid of me."

"Of course," said Paget.

"I make you nervous?"

"It's that you should leave."

"You think I'll make you pay for the bungalow, is that it?"

But he wouldn't smile. "We've got the starboard forward six-inch to bear. If the mechanism can be patched, we shall engage the enemy."

"That sounds so pompous."

"Keep away from the port-hole," he said, and left.

Mrs. Wilcox finished dicing an onion. It glistened in a heap of crystals on her chopping block. It would do for the relish. Crickington looked in.

"I believe we shall get a round off before long, Mrs. Wilcox. It might be best to keep out of harm's way."

With the blade of her heavy knife Mrs. Wilcox pushed the mound of diced onion to one side and selected one of Wrinch's bright yellow bell-peppers. "Them yellows, Mr. Wrinch is proud of them yellows."

"I should think a few bits will fall off when we fire." Crickington poked the club-end of his pitching wedge against the ceiling. "I'd want to keep a sharp eye on that, Mrs. Wilcox."

Mrs. Wilcox sliced the pepper into hemispheres, expelled the seeds with the tip of her big blade, and began to transform the crisp flesh, first into long thin strips, then into cubes. She finished off the pepper with a powerful blow, tightened her lips and stepped to the gas range. A thick green mess bubbled in an iron skillet. She sniffed at this, stirred it, went back to the chopping board. "I'll have that cuke, Mr. Crickington." She pushed the chopped pepper aside into the onions. Crickington stooped to a basket of vegetables and dug out a misshapen cucumber.

"Those six-inches, they're a nasty gun," he confided.

"I thought as you were rigging B turret," Mrs. Wilcox told the cucumber.

"Dead loss, that B turret, Mrs. Wilcox. No, it's the forward starboard six-inch. Her platform's broken, but we've spiked her round and she's almost bearing. If Sir Robert comes a few degrees to port, we shall get a shell away."

Mrs. Wilcox dispatched the cucumber, thwacking it so hard she had to yank the blade free from the wooden block. She finished chopping, and slid the minced cucumber into the pile of onion and pepper.

"Try to keep your head down, Mr. Crickington. I don't fancy mending them pants again."

He stood there clumsily, delaying as long as he could. Nothing Mrs. Wilcox could say would help him find the words he needed, or even help him know he needed them, so he left. Mrs. Wilcox stared at the mound of diced vegetables. She waited, then picked through her basket until she found some radishes. They were as large as oranges. "Mr. Wrinch is very proud of them radishes," she said to the absent Crickington, and attacked one with the knife. She finished, brushed it aside, and began to dice another. Harder and harder she chopped, faster and faster, until finally she smote the last remaining bit of radish with a furious blow that hacked into the board a whisker closer than she'd aimed, and an eighth of an inch of finger flew away.

Mrs. Wilcox gasped and dropped the knife. Blood gushed from her finger. She clamped her wrist. Blood gushed over her hand, her wrist, the fingers that clenched the wrist. The starched cuff of her blouse became a bracelet of bloody rag. She stuck the finger in her mouth, but the pain increased. She dug her fingers harder into her wrist. Blood pulsed from the severed finger. Her breath whistled through clenched teeth. She stumbled to the stove and grabbed the skillet in her uninjured hand, dumping the bubbling chutney in the sink. She found a bottle of vodka and sluiced it into the skillet. It burned off instantly, and Mrs. Wilcox jabbed her bleeding finger onto the hot metal.

"Battleship in sight!" bawled Griggs. "Enemy adrift, fine on the starboard bow!"

"Shut that man up, Guns, can't you?" cried Sir Robert. "Fellow should be in a mad house." Mrs. Wilcox had usually topped Sir Robert up by now. Damn it, a chap could die of thirst.

"*Bismarck* class!" roared Griggs.

"Of course it's the *Bismarck* class," shouted Sir Robert. "It *is* the bloody *Bismarck*!"

"She's got a German ensign at her stern," cried Griggs.

"I cannot bear this," Sir Robert ranted. "Have Crickington proceed onto the wing and silence that man by force!"

"Whunff," assented Wendy, dragging one eye open and regarding Griggs.

"Come five degrees to port, Corcoran," said Paget.

"Aye aye, sir!" yelped the rating, unnerved by Griggs and Sir Robert, and startled at the quietness of Paget's voice. "Port!" he shouted."Five degrees!"

"I am right here, Corcoran," Paget told him calmly.

"So you are, sir. Aye aye, sir."

Hood hauled slowly round to her new course. In the last hour she'd come another mile. *Bismarck* now lay five miles off. At this range a six-inch shell would strike the enemy with terrible effect – if it struck at all. *Hood*'s gun-laying and firing mechanisms were a mess of jury-rigging. The electrician's mates had wires running everywhere, taped and soldered, caught together in batches, lashed into sheaves with lengths of fishing line, carried overhead in languid loops. The electricians went at their work with manic energy. You couldn't say the same of the gunners.

Stokes-Lipton preferred to put up jam in jars. He hated Crickington, and so did Seamore the gunner's mate, who often disappeared to search the ship for swallows' eggs to trade for beer. Ferryman, Stokes-Lipton's slave, devoted his days to a quest for herbs from which he would make salves to rub on Stokes-Lipton's cracked, dry skin. These manifold concerns tended to affect the business of the guns.

"I believe the six-inch is bearing on the enemy, sir," said Paget now, raising his binoculars from the gun barrels to the German battleship, blood-red in the morning sun and ablaze with clematis.

"Eh?" said Sir Robert. He glared at Paget. "Where is that woman, Guns?" His face burned with irritation. "Are we to *wilt?*"

"Permission to open fire, sir?"

"Oh, do what you like," he shook with exasperation. "Leave me out of it, can't you?"

Paget picked up a bridge telephone. "Shoot." He waited. The gun did not fire. "Shoot," he said again. Nothing. It took a quarter-hour for Paget to locate Seamore, and five minutes more to cajole him into rounding up Stokes-Lipton.

"Certainly, sir," Seamore said obligingly, his hands full of eggs. "I shall have to find Ferryman. Mr. Stokes-Lipton won't go anywhere without that Ferryman lad."

"Very well," said Paget.

"Certainly," repeated Seamore, although he made no move to go. He stared helplessly at his eggs. Paget sighed.

"Shall I take those, Seamore?"

Paget returned to the bridge with the eggs. Seamore found Ferryman and sent him after Stokes-Lipton. One by one they trooped into the turret of the starboard forward six-inch.

"Shoot," said Paget, and a number of things happened at once.

Hans-Adam and Mimi, bound by cords made out of arms and legs, flew apart with a snap.

"Gun!" Hans-Adam cried. He stared into Mimi's face. They listened to the rising scream of the projectile followed by a sudden change in pitch. The sound receded. "I think we are hit!" Hans-Adam gasped.

"I didn't feel anything."

"It didn't explode."

"Your face is completely purple."

"Yours too."

"I never thought this would happen," Mimi said, "that they'd attack us."

"They had to."

"What are you going to do?"

In *Hood* they felt the firing throughout the ship. The six-inch gun house wrenched from its mount and leaned inboard. Stokes-Lipton and his crew lay where they fell, tumbled to one side. In their anti-flash hoods they looked like a trio of puzzled nuns whose eyes just blinked and blinked in the acrid fumes.

The vase of wildflowers jumped straight off its desk and struck Anne a blow behind the ear. "Now isn't that the dumbest thing," she told herself, and feeling a trickle of blood, grabbed the damp towel from the bed.

Wrinch gaped as a trellis fell apart. At the same time the python tumbled from his hiding place among the overhead steam pipes. He dropped like a length of cable, scales flashing as he plummeted into Wrinch's best tomatoes. This was too much for Wrinch. Arming himself with a hoe, he marched at the horrified snake. The serpent tried to thrash his way out of the wrecked vines.

"A fine thing, now," said Wrinch, and gave him a blow. The python lashed up a spray of earth and writhed frantically away, completing his devastation of the tomatoes. Wrinch watched him go. He turned to face the havoc left behind. "A fine thing," he repeated, and sat down to cry.

The Fregattenkapitän attended the sound of the six-inch gun, the rising scream of the shell, the sharp change in sound as it whined away. It's true that *Bismarck* groaned with manifold ills, and black smoke crawled about her everywhere. Also, the impact of a six-inch shell does not much trouble a 50,000-ton capital ship, even with her armor falling off in slabs, even when she is adrift, or, as her screws were turning at last, barely under way. The Fregat-tenkapitän felt the blow anyway. It intruded into a recollection of that summer at the yellow schloss – hadn't they played croquet that summer? The Fregattenkapitän made his apologies to his mother, and retreated from the lawn.

"My regrets," he murmured, although of course they'd known it would come to this.

Musikmaat Schreier snatched his violin from beneath his chin and goggled as the shell climbed swiftly across five miles of water and clubbed turret Caesar a glancing blow. Then came the awful shriek. The shell had already ricocheted away when the scream of its passage hurtled into the foretop and blasted Musikmaat Schreier to the roots of his hair. He sat down hard.

"The English have fired on me," he thought. He tried to make sense of this barbarity. What could the English want? Could they want him to play Purcell? Britten? Musikmaat Schreier did not know another English composer. He thought there were only the two. Then he became enraged. "They shoot at me because I have not played the Purcell or the Britten!? I will not play more!" He thrust his violin into its velvet case, drew up his knees and retreated into injured silence. A hundred feet below, Stabsobermaschinist Merz put an ear to the pipe and listened.

"Herr Musikmaat?" he called respectfully. He listened again. Why had he stopped playing? "Herr Musikmaat?"

Hans-Adam projected himself onto the bridge in a stream of actions strung into a single blur and ending at the chipped blue table with the panting figure of the Prince zu Westerwald, gorgeously disheveled, struggling to maintain his dignity before the frozen visage of Doña Teresa. Doña Teresa summoned all that remained of her authority, advised the Prince that his ship was under fire, commended him to his duty, slammed her visor shut and marched away.

The grey tom grinned to himself, and went to look for Mimi.

When the six-inch gun fired, a dish of relish on Mrs. Wilcox's tray flipped onto a plate of cucumber sandwiches, also on the tray. The tray was in Mrs. Wilcox's hands, and headed for Sir Robert. When it got there, Sir Robert noticed the mess. Then he noticed that Mrs. Wilcox wore a disgusting dressing and that she looked distinctly ill. He decided not to comment on any of this. A heady smell of brandy issued from the teapot, and to hell with the ancillary arrangements.

"Ah, Wendy, tea!"

Wendy had troubles of her own. The concussion of the six-inch gun had plainly disturbed her. She rose and glumly shook herself. A loose platoon of shrewlike creatures skittered in panic beneath her nose. Sickened by it all, Wendy took herself from one side of Sir Robert's chair to the other. "Broompf," she said, and sagged to the deck, and fell into a sour reverie.

"Herr Musikamaat!?" Merz called again. "Herr Musikmaat!? Will you not speak?"

In a temper Crickington clambered up to the third tee. Damn it, the third fairway was ruined. The six-inch gunhouse lay toppled right onto it. Stokes-Lipton and the others were mewling inside.

"Well I *am* sorry," said Crickington, "but it is your fault." He surveyed the fairway.

"I say," came Stokes-Lipton's muffled voice from inside the gunhouse. "Hello?"

"Oh shut up, can't you?" Crickington yelled, and swung his driver at a rabbit.

Wickel placed the two pieces of broken Meissen on his bench and turned away, for surely a gun had fired. He listened to the incoming round, felt a tremor when it struck. A hit aft, somewhere on the main battery. There was no secret *Bismarck* could hide from the Oberartilleriemechaniker. Wickel had a frame made out of iron bolts, but it encased an ardent heart. *Bismarck* he loved, and Lipp. Now one of them had taken a blow which Wickel feared must fall upon the other.

When the six-inch shell clouted turret Caesar and caromed off, it loosed a hurricane of splinters. Most of these flew overboard to pepper the surface of Lake Erie. Others scourged the ship. A hail of rusty metal hissed into the apple blossoms, where Lipp sat dreaming. A cluster of shards needled into his torso. He gasped, and his teeth fell out. His hands flew up in amazement. Groggy with pain, muddled by the drug that rummaged in his veins, Lipp tried to rise, and couldn't. He noticed his hands were wet, then saw they were stippled with blood. Wickel would be angry. Lipp found a syringe and emptied another ampoule into his leg. By the time Wickel reached him he was comfortable, only embarrassed at the mess. He clasped a blood-soaked rag which he dabbed at the worst gashes. Wickel snatched this from him in horror. Lipp raised his hands and let them fall. He smiled with his empty gums, a smile of apology.

News of the gunshot flew abroad. A line of helicopters rattled out like old jalopies and described a ragged circle around the battleships. The girl in the bomber jacket got on the horn to CNN and told them to get hold of Anne.

"What's going *on* down there?" she demanded when they patched her through.

"Oh, you know what men are like," said Anne.

"Are you trying to be *smart* with me?" demanded the girl in the bomber jacket.

"Fuck off, toots. I'm retired."

At last the partisans had something new to shout about, and into that spring morning they streamed like lapdogs after dowagers. Through the astounded lanes of Ontario they poured, Kitts and Knodler and their levies, in bakers' vans with ovens where assistants labored, preparing their arsenals, secreting nuts and bolts and bits of roofing tile in the dough, concealing their ordnance with slyly slapped-on icing decorated with every kind of sparkle and, of course, with flags. On lurched these scented caravans, until they came upon each other at the lakeside village of Erieau. Ecstatic with beer and the news of battle, the rivals fell upon each other. There beside Lake Erie on a day that rang with robins, the sky filled with volley after volley of apple strudel and banana bread.

And more.

Bakers from remote townships, irregulars without clear allegiance, men and women bent on devilry alone, began to complicate the fray with rhubarb flans sewn with lead, and a range of sinister meringues distinguished by the latest thickening agent – concrete.

xxix

LIPP LAY IN the cabin he'd shared with Wickel for fifty years. They'd not been easy years for Wickel: Lipp had a heart that wandered, and swaying hips that had wrung gasps from half the crew. But time had cured him of his crimson ways. The blunt instrument of Lipp's love had come to fall exclusively on the sick. At any scratch or headache, bruise or sprain, Lipp was sure to load his charge with handfuls of analgesic. Epp's ears had acquired their striking blueness in just this way.

Now Lipp lay in a haze himself, grateful for the blanket Wickel'd tucked around his riddled body. It was here, at Lipp's bedside, that Mimi caught up with Hans-Adam. She found him kneeling by Lipp, his head bent to the rough blanket. Lipp's cracked old fingers rested in Hans-Adam's hair. Not much compassion could survive Lipp's wounds, but whatever he could wrest from advancing narcosis and the ebb of his own life he gave. He brushed his fingers against Hans-Adam's cheek, a cheek smeared with Evening Leopard. He smiled a weary, toothless smile. His hand fell to the blanket and his eyes looked for Wickel. The Ober-artilleriemechaniker stepped forward and touched Hans-Adam's shoulder. Hans-Adam pressed his face to the blanket, then wrenched himself away. He shot a last, pathetic look at Lipp and stumbled from the cabin. Mimi followed. She touched his sleeve.

He shook off her hand. *"Now* do you understand?!" He spun away.

"Yes!" Mimi cried, hurrying after him. In a moment he'd ducked from sight. She heard him scream some words, but couldn't make them out.

Hans-Adam knew every cable on the ship, every cleat and coaming. He went through *Bismarck* like a cat. Twice Mimi caught sight of him, then tripped, banged to the deck and lost him. He dodged into hatches, swarmed up ladders, flowed forward through the ship in a blur of purpose. He reached the turret Bruno gunhouse, hauled open a hatch and dove inside. When Mimi got there she found him hurling himself among the instruments, clenching his teeth, sobbing. He thrust his eyes to the gun director, scrabbled at its controls. Useless. The sights showed only an empty view of Lake Erie and a trail of *Bismarck's* smoke, like an injured serpent, winding away to die.

"Darling," said Mimi. His sobbing frightened her. He struck the armored bulkhead with his fists, crying words she couldn't understand. Dreading the noises he made, she laid her hand against his cheek. He seized her wrist, pulling her with him as he sank to the deck.

"Lipp," he whimpered, "Lipp."

She cradled his head against her, stroking him. Slowly the shaking of his body subsided. She kissed his hair and stroked his cheek again, caressed his ears, his neck. Her hands became purple with stroking, as if this royal color were the pigment of their love. She stroked her own face too, wiping herself with care, smoothing the color across her forehead and around her eyes.

Doña Teresa helped the Fregattenkapitän into his best uniform coat. She'd brushed it till it glowed.

"You are too kind, Madame," he told her with emotion.

"Don't be silly," she replied, embarrassed.

"If the boy is anything, it is your doing," he professed, his dignity unimpaired by a trembling in his voice.

"Maybe she will take him away from us," Doña Teresa said with bitterness.

"It is to be hoped."

She pinched the bridge of her nose. "I know that I am a silly woman."

The Fregattenkapitän made himself very straight, and touched her lightly on the arm. "Your example would make your people proud."

"What do you mean?" she said dejectedly. "You are my people."

"Exactly," and Fregattenkapitän von Prenzlau caused the battle ensign to be broken out at the maintop yard. It opened to the wind with a crack that frightened the otters and made the little party gathering by turret Bruno stiffen with pride. Then the Fregattenkapitän ordered a signal: "*Bismarck* to *Hood*. Lipp is dead."

"Lipp?" goggled Stokes-Lipton when word reached him among the parsley. "Are you certain?"

"Yes," said Seamore.

"But wasn't he the gardener chap?"

"He was, sir. Yes."

Stokes-Lipton flicked his fingers at a bee. "Well that is too bad. I mean, he sent me that ointment."

"Yes."

"We threw it away."

"We did, sir. Yes."

"And now it's we who've killed him." Stokes-Lipton stared at his hands. "A chap oughtn't to have done that."

Billings, Warrenhook, and Gaspard-Smythe paused between heats. They put the turtles in the paddock and discussed Lipp in low voices.

"We should cancel the race, then?" wondered Warrenhook. And, yes, they agreed they should.

Henck went outside and kissed his jersey cow, Heidi, on her wet mouth, and told her the news. And just that way, with pagan formalities often like Henck's, the tidings of Lipp's demise went through the battleships, until everyone knew, and the vessel fortresses turned away from that dying morning into a dumbstruck afternoon, and made their courses westward. A wind in the upper reaches knotted the clouds into fantastic shapes, and sunlight licked the edges with a mustard tongue. Below, the opalescent frogs bowed their heads and raised a solemn *Dies Irae* to the sky.

And behind the ships, behind those gorgeous chromatropes of oil that stained Lake Erie like a film of glass, there rose a rumbling, a sound that shook the lake and that at last erupted in a lava-burst of words as news of Lipp's death spread. Nothing but blows would satisfy it now. The ships hobbled up their last ascent, making their way together through a closing day that seethed with smoke and the nervous calls of animals, with splendid lies, with the ravishing news of war.

XXX

THEY WRAPPED LIPP'S body in a German naval flag, weighted it with iron and shot it down a wooden slide. An otter covered its eyes as the body slapped through weeds. The vegetation closed over Lipp. Doña Teresa tore off her locket and flung it after him. It landed on the green-black weeds and glittered, until the forward passage of the ship opened a fissure in the weave of plants and the locket blinked from sight.

After the burial Musikmaat Schreier fell in with Wickel's project, already begun, of restoring turret Bruno. In warm spring sunshine the Musikmaat parked himself outside the turret, carefully, as was his way. He placed a cloth across his boots, and set to work. He received pieces of machinery, stripped the rust, oiled them, placed them on the deck. Wickel examined each piece and ticked it off on a blueprint of the firing mechanism.

Maschinenmaat Nissel set to work too. He put away his schnapps. He put away a brown 50-pfennig German (portrait of Bach). The English had murdered Lipp. There would be time for schnapps, time for the 50-pfennig, time even for a blue French commemorative of the maiden voyage of the *Normandie*, 1935, one franc fifty, which Schreier would kill for. Time for all that later. Now he took up Stabsobermaschinist Merz's crusade to supply the ship with, what, six knots of speed? Six knots became the slogan of the engine room. All of them toiled to this end. Merz toiled, Nissel toiled. Only at night did Nissel return to his schnapps, and then in the strictest moderation.

Anne stood on *Hood*'s port wing. A golden sash of cloud unfurled above Michigan. Beneath this banner, five miles ahead and wreathed in smoke, the German battleship limped into the Detroit River. She listed: her orchard looked as if it might just slide away.

A rifle sounded, and a bullet whined as it skipped off water. A girl in a boat let loose a scream, a single syllable drawn hideously out. "Liiipp!" it sounded like. She shook her rifle. Sleek heads bobbed from nearby weeds, breaking the surface in cheerful pops of light that flashed against the darker vegetation. Otters and seals turned this way and that, curious about the ricochet and the yelling girl. Anne saw the rifle go up for a second shot. Another report. A seal rolled and sank. A howl of triumph greeted this, and awakened Griggs.

"I'll give you bleeding cucumbers," he growled. "Bleeding cucumbers, bleeding relish." He raised his binoculars and swept the forward quadrants. Completing his sweep, he noticed Anne. "There's a Jerry battleship, ma'am," he told her confidentially, "bearing dead ahead." This disclosure exhausted him, and he promptly fell asleep.

Marinesignalgast Epp peered from the radio room. He did not like what he saw. Doña Teresa had eaten nothing since Epp had taken on that part of Lipp's duties. He tiptoed into the arbor and moved a saucer with his finger, to make it clatter, the way you might attract a kitten. Doña Teresa ignored him. She raised her fingers to adjust the position of her locket, but her locket was not there. Epp sucked loudly through his teeth and dug at his floppy ears with a coffee spoon. They buzzed, Epp's ears. Still, that was war. Epp made no complaint. He regarded Doña Teresa. She worried him. The Fregattenkapitän worried him. The prince too, with his purple face – all of it was worrisome. Epp banged the spoon against his ear. The buzzing stopped. He replaced the spoon and shuffled back to the radio room.

The men at work in turret Bruno didn't like the Evening Leopard on Mimi and Hans-Adam. It made them nervous. They didn't know where to look. Wickel stamped around and generally strew the deck with troubled glances. Mimi and Hans-Adam moved away in stages, first from the centre of the turret Bruno gunhouse to the edge, then through the hatch, then out as far as Schreier, and finally beyond, until they found themselves, by a process irresistible and natural, expelled entirely, a caste of two, and they wandered the last few yards to the clearing where the toy stood tethered to the deck.

"Maybe we should try to get it going," Mimi said.

"Why?"

"I don't know, why not?"

Hans-Adam cocked his head. "What's that noise?" Mimi listened too. So did the big grey tom.

"Mrrrop?" he inquired from behind a pane of shade.

No one heard him.

A ululation rose from the boats of partisans, a single syllable, intoned again and again. It came from both groups, bellowed in derision or in pride. Mimi and Hans-Adam strained to catch the word. "Liiiipp!" one fleet of boaters howled, a choir of massed imbeciles. And after a pause, the long reply: "Liiiiipp!"

xxxi

*B*ISMARCK PROCEEDED OUT of the Detroit River, crossed Lake St. Clair in a mist of petals and entered the St. Clair River. Her battle ensigns crackled. Smoke leaked out of her. The work in turret Bruno went on apace. Musikmaat Schreier uncovered diagnostic talents no one had suspected. Mimi and Hans-Adam tinkered with the toy, and once or twice it cleared its throat in a promising way, and burped. This work on the toy, because it was close to turret Bruno and was, after all, work, came to be associated with the labors on the gun itself, so that they all, toy crew and gun crew, felt yoked to a single purpose.

Wickel changed. Some of that redness left his face. If a torte should not be sweet enough (often the case), Wickel told the cooks to use more sugar. He didn't fling the rejected torte into the galley with an oath. He returned it politely, and left. This gentleness brought tears to the cook and his mates.

In this way Lipp survived, a legate to the heart of Wickel. Unable to face life without Lipp, Wickel preserved his lover in himself. He raised his hands and let them fall. He paid attention to the clematis, the orchard, to Lipp's erratic vegetables. He even fed the irascible hens, each of whom the late Matrosenhauptgefreiter had known by name.

Like an aged sister *Hood* came lumbering behind. Frankly she steered like a cow. Her bows were so far down that her rudder barely bit the water. Her pumps were losing what fight they'd had, and Wrinch kept deputizing men to steal them. Corcoran struggled to keep the battle cruiser in the upbound lane. Sir Robert slipped perilously close to dejection. Plainly Lipp's death afflicted him.

"Make a signal, should we, Guns? 'Too bad about Lipp'? Something like that?"

"I don't see how we could, sir."

"No, you are right. I cannot deny it." He slumped in his chair. Half an hour later he struggled to the surface of his misery. "Send von Prenzlau a case of something, then. We could do that, surely. What about that, eh, Guns?"

"Really, sir. They are our enemy."

"Of course they are. The Hun, what?" And Sir Robert retired to purgatory again. It was a mercy when Mrs. Wilcox arrived with a tray. Sir Robert helped himself to tea so stiff with rum it could have bounced. It seemed to revive him, and he tipped a sandwich to the deck. The dog Wendy regarded it, allowed an expression of bottomless resignation to drag at her features, then sucked the sandwich back with a tired "flumpf!"

"You're extremely pale, Mrs. Wilcox," Crickington observed, with some embarrassment. "Hadn't you to have that looked at?"

Mrs. Wilcox examined her bandage, now stained by relish. "Sir Robert's lost his appetite."

"To hell with Sir Robert!"

"Now, now, Mr. Crickington," she whispered.

Crickington went forward in a rage and began to attack the partisans. They jammed the waterway — excellent targets for a man with a driver and a basket of iron chunks. Enormous golf pants snapped at his legs.

"Lipp! Lipp! Lipp!" they chanted.

"Lipp, is it? I'll give you Lipp," cried Crickington, and he whacked away. A murderous rain pattered into boats and motor yachts. Some cheered; some waved their fists: all were at risk and many injured by Crickington's enfilade. No one fled. Nothing could seduce them from that swill of passion.

"Lipp!"

Raucous cavalcades poured through the landscape of Ontario. Miles of campgrounds and motels fell to them. Yards of strudel laced with razor wire. Banana bread rigged to explode at a touch. Epp followed it all. Reports chattered out on printers in his radio room. He read them, stapled them together, brought them out to Doña Teresa. Perhaps the news might prod her appetite. There were plenty of tinned peaches left. Epp had looked.

"Take it away," she told him when he laid his stapled bundle by her cup. "They are nothing, these people."

He returned disheartened to the radio room and subdued his ears with some soldering wire. Inch by inch the news streamed out around him, paragraph by paragraph. War came to the low, round hillsides of Ontario, revelry and war.

Crickington smacked another lump of metal at the boaters. A gash appeared on the forehead of a partisan. Crickington grinned and shoved the driver back in his bag. He hoisted his clubs and made his way to A turret. It was Crickington's responsibility to supervise the gunners and machinists charged with refurbishing the gun. He found them milling about in confusion. The problem seemed to be Stokes-Lipton.

"I mean," Stokes-Lipton was telling Seamore, "if we're going to be killing chaps, well I mean, I don't think I care for it."

Crickington put down his bag, fished out the four-iron, and

took a swipe at Stokes-Lipton's ankles. The mutiny ended. Now the gunhouse hummed to the ministrations of technicians. Stokes-Lipton himself checked the elevation system. Seamore attacked the optics. Ferryman was licensed to forage for medicines to ease Stokes-Lipton's pains. Crickington saw that it all got under way. Then he went forward with another basket of iron. A boat ploughed through the weeds alongside, and called the name of Lipp, and Crickington planted his tee.

Up the channel went the battle cruiser *Hood*. The work in A turret stopped for a picnic on deck. They fed their scraps to gulls, and went back to work. In the power plant they labored too, patching and nursing the furnaces. Nearby, grateful for warmth, the old jaguars lay on greasy blankets. Mice scampered across those ruined paws. The jaguars dreamt of green leaves and snakes with skin like diamonds. Elderly stokers brought bowls of milk-soaked bread and placed them by the cats, who ate a little and returned to sleep.

In line ahead the warships entered Lake Huron and settled on a northerly course. The men felt better when their ships gained wider waters. It was pleasant to be working. Stokes-Lipton snapped at Ferryman, which frankly Ferryman enjoyed.

A cloud of ruby-throated hummingbirds swept aboard without warning and fanned out to comb the ship. "Guns," cried Sir Robert. "*Archilochus colubris!*"

Paget pursed his lips and trained his glasses on some flowers forward. There they were. "Fifty-five wingbeats a second when they hover," he recited. "More when they move."

"All the way from South America!"

Paget nodded. "Males arrive first."

"Voracious little folk," Sir Robert chuckled. "They've a passion for spiders, a passion." The hummingbirds would not stay, but began to drift away in groups. In a panic Sir Robert ordered bowls of sugared water placed about the ship. To no avail. Soon the last of them darted off, watched by Sir Robert, Paget, Anne: specks of colored feather vanishing into streaks of smoke.

"The Germans seem to be on fire," said Anne.

"We both are, actually." Paget put his glasses down. "You've hurt yourself."

"It's not bleeding, is it?" she touched the place where the vase had struck.

"Be a splendid bruise. Mind you don't frighten the children."

Anne gave him a long look. "Did you just make a joke?"

Paget raised his binoculars and trained them on *Bismarck*. "So it would appear."

Anne pulled his head down by the ears and kissed him on the lips. "I can't stand much more of this, big guy. I'm warning you." Back in the cabin she tried Mimi's number.

"Hello?"

"Palango, you're on fire."

"I know. It stinks. They say we're not going to sink, though."

"Great. As long as everything's fine, I guess I can get back to my ironing."

"We're working on the toy again."

"Oh, good. I'll fill everybody in here, because as far as I know they're still operating on the old plan, the one where we batter you to death."

"I know it sounds insane. But it's brought him closer to me."

"It does sound insane, Mimi. Also, it *is* insane."

"I can't explain it."

"Well I can." Anne's fax beeped. A message from archives started curling out. Anne scooped up the machine and launched it through the window. "Once you step inside somebody else's story, the logic of that story takes over. It's why war correspondents are corrupt. They have no place to go that's outside the war. Even if they criticize it, they criticize it on its own terms." She searched for a cigar, whacking a pile of faxes from the desk. "I hope you're listening, because this is a terrific speech."

"I have to get back soon."

"Let me put it another way: If you don't get off you're going to die."

"I thought you were all zen about this."

"Except when I panic."

"I totally love him, Desirée."

"It's nuts, Palango."

"It's my destiny."

Anne blinked back tears. "That's what I'm afraid of, Red."

"Don't tell me you're crying."

"Don't worry. I won't tell you."

"This is our story, Desirée."

"Well," Anne sniveled, "I guess you know I love you."

And there were those words again, ensigns themselves, raised hopelessly against that pestilence that spilled from town to shore, from shore to the middle reaches of the lake, to *Bismarck*'s skirt of weed, to that howling fracas of opposing boats, to the black smoke that leaked from the battleships and drifted off to starboard, where it hung until the westerly chewed it into haze.

xxxii

"SHE'S BARELY ANSWERING, sir," said Corcoran. "I should think she has scarcely any rudder," Paget replied. "Her nose is damn near under."

"That she is, sir."

"Crickington, get back aft with some of the hands. My compliments to Mr. Wrinch, and I'll have a dozen of those pumps."

Crickington grinned, and swiped his four-iron in pure joy. "Wrinch won't like that."

"I daresay," Paget said, and a rain of metal splinters came inboard from a fusillade. Sir Robert surfaced long enough to direct a sneer overboard. "Put a round into them, Guns, what?"

Paget stared at Anne's cheek. A splinter had opened a three-inch gash. His own chin was speckled with blood from the violence of Anne's laceration.

"You're hit!" she exclaimed.

"I'm afraid not," said Paget evenly.

Anne's face just flopped, as if a string that tied it all together had been cut. She looked into Paget's eyes as she felt the warmth of her own blood on her cheek and neck. "Me?"

"So it would appear."

Anne's lips turned white. The first tremor of shock fluttered onto her face. "I don't want to touch it," she said.

"You, there," Paget snapped at Griggs.

"Eh!?" the yeoman jumped.

"My compliments to Mr. Ismay, and he will report to the bridge at once."

"I'm bleeding all over myself," Anne giggled.

Paget looked at her sharply, then pressed a handkerchief to her cheek. "It's only a nick."

"More of those skirmishers on the port beam, Guns," drawled Sir Robert from behind binoculars. The attack seemed to revive him.

Ten minutes later Ismay appeared – a small, blackish figure. "Let's have him on the deck, then," he told Paget.

"Her," said Paget.

"Eh?"

"A lady," Paget explained.

"I know all that," Ismay said reprovingly. "Let's have him on the deck," he repeated, severely this time, as if Paget had questioned his medical authority. They helped Anne to the deck. She winked at Paget, then started to blubber. "I know all that," murmured Ismay. He knelt beside her and lifted Paget's handkerchief from the wound. "Very nice," he pronounced. "Tidy, no dirt. You're lucky, my lad."

Later a soft spring snow, elaborate and calm, coasted out of the sky. Veiled by enormous flakes the great ships made their way. The snowfall mantled their decrepitude. In silhouette they returned to that old dream of warfare, of iron cities arrayed in battle order, ensigns and pennants and signals streaming, standing on toward the enemy.

The snow did not cease until day bled into evening, when it fell off suddenly. A livid sky flared up and bathed the ships in a farewell bath of gold and red. Lake Huron shone like a lake of scarlet ink in that last breath before the sun sank into Michigan. Now the warships ascended in darkness. Neither ship wore running lights. Here and there in those iron cliffsides burned a yellow cabin light, pulsing and fading. The thrum of crippled engines filled water and black sky. Two castellated towns moved up Lake Huron in the night, with choruses of chanting frogs. Bilges swarmed with hunting animals and prey. All proceeded to that ancient, muffled beat of war, as with mouse and python, rabbit, bat, and bird, Birnam Wood sailed slowly up to Dunsinane.

xxxiii

MIMI AND HANS-ADAM lay enclosed in the irresistible inertia of the ship. They breathed each other's body scent, and the smell of bunker oil. This perfume washed them like a blood-warm sea. They floated in it.

"I hardly remember who I am," said Mimi. She traced her finger through the purple stubble of his jaw.

Flames jumped onto the ceiling as a bottle of gas exploded on the hull. Mimi kissed his eyes. Her arm lay over him.

"I was six years old," Hans-Adam said, and he told her about the man who'd come to the chapel at Westerwald to search the tablets. He found the one that told how Prince Klaus-Franz-Maria, on duty in the after fire-control position of the battleship *Bismarck*, had on 27 May, 1941, in an engagement commencing at 8:47 in the morning and lasting almost two hours, survived broadside after broadside from the battleships *Rodney* and *King George V*, had returned to Westerwald an invalid, and died there Christmas Day, year of our Lord one thousand nine hundred and sixty-three, in the forty-eighth year of his age.

"Well," the Fregattenkapitän had said, "I knew him, your papa."

"Prince Klaus," the boy had piped.

"Kapitänleutnant Prince zu Westerwald," the Fregattenkapitän had pronounced in a dreamy voice.

And in the present Mimi asked: "Did he ever make you a special machine of your own?"

"He taught me to fish." Prince Klaus in a bath chair with a blanket around his legs. "He smoked, and threw his cigarettes on the grass. A footman followed to pick them up."

"And you learned to fish?"

"I learned to ruin fly-rods by beating them against the ground."

"He didn't get mad?"

"Raise the arm slowly but steadily to eleven o'clock." Prince Klaus discarded another cigarette. "Then advance it slowly but steadily to one o'clock."

Hans-Adam had thrashed solemnly about, whipping the practice fly onto the grass behind him, lashing it forward onto the lake.

"Excellent," his father'd said, "and if that doesn't work, we'll use grenades."

A scream returned them to Lake Huron. More flamelight on the ceiling: another bottle of gas. Hans-Adam rolled onto his back. The flames died out. It became pitch black. Water gurgled alongside. A nightbird made a call close by. Out of the night arose a distant and remorseless incantation:

"Lipp! Lipp! Lipp!"

Mimi knew from a felt motion Hans-Adam was tapping his fingernail against his teeth. She moved against him. He stiffened, only slightly, but as violent to Mimi as a blow.

"I hate them too," she made her voice calm.

"Of course."

"Don't say it like that. Aren't I in this too?"

"I'm perhaps more in it than you."

"I wish you wouldn't say that. I thought we were choosing to be together."

Hans-Adam drew a long, slow breath and let it out. "You can't choose everything in life. It doesn't work like that."

"What's that supposed to mean?" She grabbed his arm. "You always do this! Why does everything have to be some kind of haunted forest!?"

Hans-Adam looked away. "I hate it when you're like this."

"What do you mean, like *this*?" She jumped to her knees and ripped away the covers. Wings fluttered in a corner: a blue jay burst for the porthole with a raucous cry. Hans-Adam passed directly from surprise to anger.

"You really are tiresome!"

Spark to kindling.

Mimi yanked the pillow from beneath his head and swung it at his face, a cruel blow, and she would have repeated it if Hans-Adam hadn't wrenched the pillow from her and hurled it away. She attacked him with her fists. A blow caught him on the mouth, splitting his lower lip. He struck her with his open hand. This stopped them. Dumbfounded by their violence, they reeled to their feet.

"Oh, baby," whispered Mimi. She reached for him. He parried her hand and quickly began to dress. "We can't do this," said Mimi, clawing a sheet around her. Hans-Adam shook his head, slipped into a shirt, found his shoes. Twice he stopped to wipe blood from his chin. He gave Mimi a smile remembered from his father's face, of perfect carelessness, a smile that wanted nothing. Mimi clutched the sheet and watched him go, and refused to cry, refused.

The cabin filled with a shell-pink dawn.

The tom came gliding in. From his sun-sized yellow eyes he stared at her.

"Come here, you," Mimi wept, digging at her tears with a wad of sheet.

But the tom turned wordlessly away.

Anne woke to the same pink dawn. A throb in her cheek reminded her of her wound. Gingerly she touched the dressing. A gust of smoke blew by, a shouted "Lipp!" *Hood*'s engines mumbled far below; water bubbled alongside. The tinkle of a cup and saucer announced Mrs. Wilcox.

"You'll be wanting coffee, I expect." She made a shooing sound at a rabbit, which wrinkled its nose and went on chewing. Mrs. Wilcox set her tray on the bedside table.

"You look pretty much like hell," said Anne, sitting up.

"It's a proper coffee," Mrs. Wilcox pronounced in a shaky voice. Her lips trembled, grey in a grey face.

"Sit here," said Anne, patting the bunk.

Mrs. Wilcox obeyed. "I can't find them sandwich things."

"You need a doctor," said Anne.

"Sir Robert will be wanting his tea."

"Sir Robert is a decrepit alcoholic," Anne said cheerfully. The throb of her wound elated her. Its steady beat of pain reminded her body of its essential health. She slipped aside and pushed Mrs. Wilcox into the pillows.

"He'll be wanting that tea," worried Mrs. Wilcox.

Anne put a hand to Mrs. Wilcox's forehead. "You're burning up."

Paget was on the port wing surveying the movements of the partisans. "Up and about, then?" he said when Anne stepped out.

"I'm not the one who needs a doctor." She explained about Mrs. Wilcox.

"Griggs," called Paget. "My compliments to Mr. Ismay, and we require him."

Griggs looked blankly at Paget, wrestled for a moment with the twin notions of compliments and Ismay, and pottered off. Anne took Paget's binoculars and scanned the ragtag boats. "I didn't think I could hate people so much."

Paget shrugged. "They are who they are."

She handed back the binoculars, "I may have to kiss you again."

"Ah, Ismay," said Paget as the surgeon came scowling up behind Griggs.

"I know all that," said Ismay. "Chap's dressing wants changing." He glared at Paget, assessing him with full responsibility for the dressing, the wound, for Ismay's amazingly oily skin. "Let's have you on the deck, my lad," he ordered Anne. Later he attended Mrs. Wilcox. Plainly her infected finger horrified him. He emptied a syringe of morphine into her and set about repairing the stinking mess. He left her with a fresh white dressing that bulbed out like a bandaged grapefruit. He entrusted Anne with a palmful of pills.

"Five of these a day, mind, and I don't want him out of that bed."

"She's worried we can't get along without her," said Anne.

"I know all that," Ismay said dismissively, and left.

"What a fuss," said groggy Mrs. Wilcox.

"Boodla-boodla-boodla," went the phone, "boodla-boodla-boodla." Anne picked it up.

"I've really done it this time," said Mimi. "I slugged him."

"That's OK. It'll get his attention."

"He's disappeared."

"Track him down by smell, Palango. He's sure to be trailing musk."

"That Palango tart, she's useless. She's behaving like a wiener."

"You'll have to kill her. This is the wisdom of the moment."

"I'm standing here in a sheet. Do you think we're crazy?"

"No, I think *you're* crazy. I'm already dressed." Anne closed the mouthpiece, walked lightly to the porthole, dropped the phone over the side. She returned to sit by Mrs. Wilcox. "I should have done that long ago. She's a big girl."

"I hope Mr. Crickington hasn't made a mess of them clean pants," worried Mrs. Wilcox, a last, loyal worry before sleep. Anne tugged a blanket into place.

"If I left," Anne asked the sleeping Mrs. Wilcox, "where would I go?"

xxxiv

M IMI SEARCHED FIRST at turret Bruno. No one had seen Hans-Adam. She checked the orchard. Only Heidi moved among the apple trees, snuffling at tufts of grass, pulling out weeds and chewing ruminatively, gazing at Mimi out of huge brown eyes. Mimi didn't think she'd find him on the bridge, but tried. Epp silenced his buzzing ear with a pair of tin snips, and shook his head. Mimi sat down hopelessly at the chipped blue table.

"I can't find him. We had an awful fight."

Doña Teresa moved her fingertip against her blouse. "The enemy are trying to kill us, you see."

Bismarck stood northwards up the lake. Wickel's team hammered away at turret Bruno. Epp brought coffee in a silver pot. The Meissen cup looked good as new.

"I shouldn't have hit him. I had no right to do that."

Doña Teresa wished she would go away. A crackle of small arms attracted her glance. A bullet pinged close by. Those dreadful boats were potting at them. Still, it was lovely here. Doña Teresa decided not to mind the smoke. The fires would burn out. A breeze blew through every crack and some kind of finch had flown out to colonize the pink *montana*. It was too bad the girl must droop. Doña Teresa supposed the dispute to be beyond repair. "You will get sad-lines on your face," she said.

"He's not working on the gun. He's not at the toy. He's not in the orchard. He's not *here*."

Musikmaat Schreier brought the news. He advanced carefully onto the bridge, picking his way through the surviving bees. He drew himself up before the chipped blue table. The Prince zu Westerwald had taken himself into the foretop with a pair of Lugers and a box of old grenades. "He will not to come down," the Musikmaat judged.

"You talked to him?"

The Musikmaat admitted he had not, but had formed this impression by observing how Kapitänleutnant Prince zu Westerwald was heaving grenades at the partisans.

"His duty," said Doña Teresa, adjusting the position of a unit of space once occupied by her locket.

Mimi wouldn't wait for even the barest directions. She dashed away into that tangle of hatches and ladders behind the bridge. For an hour she clambered up through ducts and shattered corridors. A colony of squirrels screamed at her and fled into some pipes. A flabbergasted shrike rose from its nest in high alarm. Her way ran into hatches fused by rust. She retraced her steps a dozen times. Once she came to a patch of moss and ferns. It sagged when she stepped on it, and her foot broke through. A gust of oily air followed her leg when she pulled it out. A metal snag sliced her ankle open.

A crenellation of upright remnants surrounded what remained of *Bismarck*'s foretop. Hans-Adam sat on the deck with his knees drawn up, his back resting against a section of outer wall. His eyes were closed and his arms stretched forward, wrists resting on his knees. A Luger dangled in his right hand. A volley of bullets pattered against the steel bulwark. Hans-Adam opened his eyes and saw her. He closed his eyes again.

"Celestina Villahermosa," said Mimi, crawling across the deck on her hands and knees. "I'm doing a story on weapons-grade sex. They sent me up here."

"What magazine did you say you were with?" Hans-Adam asked, his eyes still closed.

"*Travel & Leisure*," she pulled herself into the shelter of the steel. "I've promised the Palango woman an exclusive."

"That harlot. She's using you."

"She'll break my heart."

"She'll spell your name wrong."

"I guess you didn't bring any food."

"I ordered a magnum of Mumms. It should be here any minute."

"Nothing to eat?"

"You can eat anything with Mumms," said Mimi, "even me."

"Madame is too modest."

"Please, call me Celestina."

Another fusillade spattered against the steel. They felt it pinging in their spines. Hans-Adam smacked the butt of his Luger. An empty magazine clattered to the deck. He inserted a fresh clip and shoved it home. He glanced at Mimi and rolled away to an opening. Mimi snatched a look at her ankle. The sight of the wound, the fact of it, embarrassed her. At least it had stopped bleeding. She crawled to Hans-Adam.

A rush of vertigo dizzied her when she looked down. A Lilliputian Musikmaat Schreier, his microscopic boots twinkling in the sunshine, made his way to turret Bruno. All of Lake Huron reached away, immense. To the left lay Michigan. On the right, beyond a line of beach and pale cliffs, of tin-roofed barns and neat, self-conscious towns, Ontario stretched off to a green horizon.

The battleship advanced through the freshwater sea. Her ship's breath skidded through the stack. Smoke blew from a dozen places where incendiary bombs had found debris. The skirt of vegetation undulated on the water. Otters kept a wary eye on the baying humans packed around.

Boatloads of them. Cabin cruisers coursed insanely up and down, heaving their wakes into the opalescent frogs. Exuberantly drunk, the boaters howled and waved and jerked their hips. Scores of them converged on *Bismarck*, hundreds. Kayaks and rubber dinghies. Men in narrow launches, purposeful, holding their bows into the swell as they aimed rifles at the rusted fortress that went sliding by, her battle ensigns blowing languidly ten storeys up.

Hans-Adam poked the barrel of his Luger through a gap and fired rapidly. Mimi winced.

"If you've got any rocks or anything for me to throw, I ask only to serve the Fatherland."

"I saw your ankle," he told her, brushing aside her banter.

A rush of pure relief built up behind her eyes. "I didn't know where you'd gone."

"Please don't cry, Mimi."

"There's nothing wrong," she sobbed. "It's OK."

He shifted himself and put his arm around her. She trembled. "It's only a gash," he said. "Wickel will know what to do."

"Don't I get a brandy?"

"Yes, if we decide to amputate."

An ensign rippled lazily, enormously, laying itself out along the breeze. Mimi shivered, a spasm violent enough to make her teeth click. He held her more tightly, and studied the weapon in his hand. "It's not easy to know what to do."

"Maybe I'm what you're supposed to do."

He surveyed the lake, the mass of enemies that dogged his ship. He studied his own hand, stained purple. He waved the pistol. "It's not a life I can walk out of easily."

"Uneasily, then."

"And become what?" He tapped the barrel of the pistol against his teeth, once, very lightly, absently. Mimi placed a finger against the barrel and pushed it away from his face. Hans-Adam sighed. "You're getting pale. I'll have to take you down."

"What some women won't do."

"I have to say I do love you," the Prince zu Westerwald confessed, sadly, as he tucked his gun away and dragged Mimi to the hatch. He climbed down the ladder, hooked his leg through a rung, and guided her legs into place on either side of his neck, taking her weight on his shoulders as she slid down.

"Tell the truth," said Mimi weakly. "You adore this."

"It's my fault."

"It's always the man's fault."

It took two hours to wind their way from foretop to bridge. Somewhere in that journey Mimi and Hans-Adam accepted the hopelessness of their condition, the condition of love. Later Wickel sluiced a bucket of disinfectant onto Mimi's leg, swaddled it in bandage, raised his hands and let them fall. Evening came on. Musikmaat Schreier reported with his violin, and unstrung a line of Schubert. The otters blinked and settled deeper in the weeds. The frogs attended Schubert gravely. Mimi and Hans-Adam went to sit in the orchard. Fires burned on the water. Fire barges prowled along the weeds. Attendants nursed the flames. Sometimes they launched in marvelously quick succession a stream of brands that arced through the sky. They tried again to ignite the slick around the battleship. Fires browsed along the edges, lazily absorbing smaller flames that blew in fitful tufts of green and blue and white.

"What are we going to do about the toy?" asked Mimi.

"We should get it to work."

"When would we lie in it, though?"

"Anytime."

"It wouldn't seem right, would it, when you're having a war?"

Hans-Adam raised his eyebrows. "We can't be serious all the time, Mimi."

She took his hand. "I wonder if we'd be happier if things were different."

"Well, you would wonder that anyway."

Five miles back, *Hood* too had fires grazing at her sides, and firelight flickered from a dozen places on the battle cruiser. The ships sailed up Lake Huron in the night, apple trees aquiver in the breeze, someone sewing buttons somewhere, someone yawning behind battlements that rose against the stars.

XXXV

A LL NEXT MORNING the warships sailed north. At noon they reached the latitude of Cape Hurd and altered course, first *Bismarck*, then *Hood*. They put their bows northeast, then east, and so came into Georgian Bay by the channel that lies to the north of Cove Island.

Through one whole afternoon they crossed the great bay, closing the eastern shore – a rocky coast strewn with an archipelago of thirty thousand islands. A stiffening breeze out of west-northwest scraped off the partisans and cleared the ships of smoke, blowing it away in sheets of ochre and brown. The battle ensigns stood out like boards, which cheered the men. Even Stokes-Lipton's vassal, Ferryman, managed to cock his head. This astonished Stokes-Lipton, who forgot to berate Ferryman for lateness with the salve. Seamore cleared his throat and grinned at his hands. Only Wrinch remained morose, and Billings, Warrenhook and Gaspard-Smythe. An incendiary bursting in the turtle pens had burned the turtles badly, and they'd had to be put down. Still, musn't complain. War, what?

Anne appeared in black pants and a loose white shirt. Her hair was pulled back, she wore pearl earrings, her cheek had a smaller bandage. "We're not as young as we used to be, Paget," she said in a companionable way, and took out her cigars.

"You're very pretty," said Paget.

"Careful, now. I might have to muss your hair."

Two bonfires bobbed together a mile to starboard. Paget took a moment to light his cigar. He studied the distant flames. "Persistent chaps."

"It's hopeless, isn't it?" said Anne, her cigar tweezered in a holder made of knuckles, the smoke curling up and wreathing her faraway face. "It's not as if you think there's anything heroic about it."

"No question of that," Paget agreed. A fire detonated cans of paint in a locker somewhere forward, sending a quiver through the deck. Paget admired the tip of his cigar. "They're good, these."

"You never said that before, that I look pretty."

"Yes, well, you do."

Wrinch went blackly through the ship, his eyes glittering through eyebrows. He let his shipmates understand that nothing was less certain than their supply of produce.

"No pumps, no water. No water, no tomatoes. You might want to think about that as you play about with them guns." He swiveled his torso in one direction, then another. No one listened. "It'll be tins for supper," grunted Wrinch.

On the bridge they could not suppress their spirits. Things looked promising in A turret. Mrs. Wilcox dug out Sir Robert's best uniform, and Crickington's. She brushed them down. In a chest she found white shirts, and ironed them. She wouldn't hear of bed.

"Mr. Ismay has put me *that* right," she declared, and unearthed a dark blue dress and a pair of black pumps.

"I say. Rather decent, Mrs. Wilcox," said Crickington, and Mrs. Wilcox buried a scarlet face among the tea things.

The Fregattenkapitän and Doña Teresa, Hans-Adam and Mimi dined by candlelight. A snowy cloth covered the chipped blue table. They all admired how the rocky islands retained a pinkish glow after sunset. Wickel tripped in with a decanter of brandy and a Lipp-like smile. He bobbed around the table, fussed with dishes, and withdrew.

"I wish he would shout at someone," said Doña Teresa, but she said it softly.

"He's replaced my bandage twice," said Mimi, and squeezed Hans-Adam's hand. Doña Teresa suppressed a shudder of irritation and tipped a slug of brandy into the peaches, peaches fresh from the tin. She ladled precisely two of these into a shallow dish and placed it beside the Fregattenkapitän's sterling silver spoon.

"Ah," he breathed.

Marinesignalgast Epp, awkward in his best uniform, came onto the bridge on a pretext of delivering the news.

"You look splendid," Doña Teresa told him. Musikmaat Schreier presented himself as well, and soon a passage of Schubert was drifting out to melt on a scent of pines. "I suppose they shall all be ruined," said Doña Teresa tightly, determined that her voice would not shake, "all our magnificent men."

"Madame," said the Fregattenkapitän.

"I know," she said.

And night swept up upon them in a surge of stars.

In the morning the partisans returned. They swarmed out from marinas on the coast, poured through the islands screaming their anthem: "Lipp!" CNN buzzed out for a last look. The girl in the bomber jacket hung in the open hatch so the airstream would suck her hair straight out. That's how the battleships appeared on TV: behind the girl in the bomber jacket, behind her hair.

Larry King decided to pass on the ships. Hey, who would call in who wasn't there already?

A frieze of vermilion cumulus ran ruler-straight above the land. Henck gazed at it as he tethered Heidi aft of turret Caesar. He stroked her flank. She dropped her head into a patch of foot-high clover; Henck breathed deeply, once, and took himself inside to lay his useless gunsight onto *Hood*.

Mimi stopped looking for the tom, *made* herself stop looking.

Wrinch reconciled himself to the pumps. He'd never get them now; the bows were as good as under. He regarded his silent gardens and he thought, it will go hard on the tomatoes.

Petals streamed from the clematis, clouds of rose and yellow and magenta. A threadbare detachment of bees went mumblingly about, confused by the rain of bombs and the thud of igniting oil. The otters kept their nerve, and the banded snakes exhibited disdain for the yelling partisans.

Now *Bismarck* came onto a northerly course, and *Hood* behind, their battle ensigns furling and unfurling high above. And they went like that, old enemies together, into a stone country where the only smells were the smells of water and pines, and also smoke. On they sailed, into that shining day and toward what lay beyond – a golden afternoon, a violet evening, into the purple duchy of the night.